The K

CW00556177

Copyright © 1998 Johnny Rogan

Edited by Chris Charlesworth
Cover & Book designed by Hilite Design & Reprographics Limited
Picture research by Nikki Russell

ISBN: 0.7119.6314.2
Order No: OP47877

Exclusive Distributors:
Book Sales Limited, 8/9 Frith Street, London W1V 5TZ, UK.
Music Sales Corporation, 257 Park Avenue South, New York, NY 10010, USA.
Five Mile Press, 22 Summit Road, Nobie Park, Victoria 3174, Australia.

To the Music Trade only:
Music Sales Limited, 8/9, Frith Street, London W1V 5TZ, UK.

Photo credits: Front cover: Rex. All other pictures supplied by Harry Goodwin and LFI.

Every effort has been made to trace the copyright holders of the photographs in this book but one or two were unreachable. We would be grateful if the photographers concerned would contact us.

Printed in Great Britain by Printwise (Haverhill) Limited, Suffolk

A catalogue record for this book is available from the British Library.

Visit Omnibus Press at http://www.omnibuspress.com

OMNIBUS PRESS
LONDON · NEW YORK · SYDNEY

CONTENTS

INTRODUCTION

With a catalogue of this size, there is no space to spare for lengthy acknowledgements, introductions or potted histories. Suffice to say, this is a track by track analysis of the Kinks' recorded works. Serial numbers and release dates are of UK origin, unless otherwise stated.

Many thanks to four fellow Kinks aficianados Keith Rodger, Doug Hinman, Peter Doggett and Russell Smith. Over the years, I have interviewed many members of the Kinks, plus their ex-managers, producers and associates. All have helped to provide some of the information or perspectives herein, not to mention the backbone of my previous book on the Kinks *The Sound And The Fury* and the extensively updated version printed in Japan during 1995.

JOHNNY ROGAN

SINGLES:
THE PYE YEARS
1964-1971

During the Sixties, the Kinks' catalogue was divided neatly between singles, EPs and albums releases. The majority of their classic hits were not included on official LPs but instead appeared either on EPs or a hotch potch of cheap compilation albums, many of which were rapidly deleted or repackaged. In common with the Rolling Stones book in this series I am therefore isolating the group's Sixties single and EP releases for separate appraisal as these represent the cornerstone of the Kinks' recording legacy. After 1970, the Kinks' singles releases almost invariably featured tracks available on contemporaneous albums. One significant exception was the 1977 festive single 'Father Chrismas'/'Prince Of The Punks' (Arista ARISTA 153).

Although the CD age has produced a variety of Kinks' compilations, these have been spread across different reissue labels. Readers wishing to find a CD that includes the singles releases from the Sixties have been faced with an array of generally unsatisfactory releases, many of which have already been deleted. The most inclusive CD compilation was the two volume *Complete Singles Collection 1964-1966* and *Complete Singles Collection 1967-1970*, which neatly catalogued the Pye years. Unfortunately, this was a Japanese release, which remains unissued in the UK/US market and was itself deleted during the early Nineties. Charly Records still market *Fab Forty – The Singles Collection 1964-1970*, which duplicates much of the Japanese release, but misses some crucial tracks, most notably 'Dedicated Follower Of Fashion' and 'Drivin''. It should also be noted that 'Lola' is the LP rather than single version.

Castle Communications have recently issued *The Singles Collection/Waterloo Sunset* (Essential ESSCD 592), which at least rounds up the Kinks and Dave Davies A-sides from this golden age period. If a B-side compilation followed (an unlikely occurrence) then the group's Sixties' catalogue, which included many sterling flip sides, would at last be well served on CD. However, it hardly needs stressing that anyone wishing to hear the sound of the Kinks in their greatest glory needs to track down the original 45s from the Sixties period. The singles retain a power and resonance, the beauty of which is unlikely ever to be captured on CD.

LONG TALL SALLY/I TOOK MY BABY HOME
RELEASED: FEBRUARY 1964
ORIGINAL UK ISSUE: PYE 7N 15611

The Kinks' debut single was an opportunist cover of Little Richard's 'Long Tall Sally'. Promoter Arthur Howes had put through an urgent call to the group's manager Larry Page after witnessing the Beatles' version of the song at the Paris Olympia on 17 January. It was hoped that the group might cash in on the Merseybeat craze, but their cover lacked passion. On reflection, it did well to reach number 42 in *Melody Maker*, although it was conspicuously absent from every other chart. "Dave would have been better singing it," his brother admitted. "He was the Little Richard expert in the band."

The flip side, written by Ray Davies, was another attempt at Merseybeat-style R&B, backed by piano and some surprising Beach Boys-influenced harmonies. Only three Kinks played on the single – their new drummer Mick Avory was replaced by the well-known session man, Bobby Graham.

YOU STILL WANT ME/YOU DO SOMETHING TO ME
RELEASED: APRIL 1964
ORIGINAL UK ISSUE: PYE 7N 15636

These tracks were recorded at the same session as their first single and were issued while the group was touring. 'You Still Want Me' again revealed a strong Beatles' influence as well as suggesting Ray's ability as a copyist. Under supervision from his managers, he hid his North London accent and sang as though he were a Liverpudlian with elocution lessons.

The B-side was another workmanlike beat ballad with banal lyrics. Avory was once again absent and the single proved the worst selling of any in the group's history. As Dave Davies told me: "I never liked those early recordings. We had a rough sound and when we'd get in the studio it would be all smoothed out."

YOU REALLY GOT ME/ IT'S ALRIGHT
RELEASED: AUGUST 1964
ORIGINAL UK ISSUE: PYE 7N 15673

The Kinks' crucial third single was a story in itself. Dave Davies had been experimenting with distortion on his guitar, an effect that he produced by piercing his speakers with knitting needles and lacerating the equipment with a razor blade. The sound was unique, with a raw, metallic edge missing from their previous singles. Unfortunately, their initial attempt at recording the song with producer Shel Talmy proved disappointing. "The original was flooded with echo and they wanted a much drier recording that was less produced," recalls manager Robert Wace. "Ray was so sure that the recording of 'You Really Got Me' was terrible and wouldn't be successful that I personally paid for it to be re-recorded at IBC. He was saying that if it went out he'd pack it in." The second version, which also featured drummer Bobby Graham, was a tense affair which brought out the best in Dave Davies. "It was a great experience standing next to Dave when he played that," Ray remembered. "I was shouting at him, willing him to do it, saying it was the last chance we had. There's determination, fight and guts in that record. 'You Really Got Me' was, in a way, a computerised versions of all we were doing."

The B-side, 'It's Alright' was an even earlier song that the group had previously recorded as a demo under their former name, the Ravens. With a predictable harmonica opening, this was a typical R&B shouter backed by a metronome riff.

ALL DAY AND ALL OF THE NIGHT/I GOTTA MOVE
RELEASED: OCTOBER 1964
ORIGINAL UK ISSUE: PYE 7N 15714

With pressure to repeat the success of 'You Really Got Me', the Kinks came up with a record that was at once a copy of its predecessor and subtly different enough to stand in its right as an arguably superior follow-up. Dave

Davies offered one of his rawest, most chaotic solos, characterized by those abrupt chord changes and a slightly stronger melody line. Ray also provided one of his better lyrics, with an instantly engaging opening that combined frustration with emotional possessiveness: "I'm not content to be with you in the daytime". Later covered by countless garage groups and subsequently a hit for the Stranglers, no version has come close to the Kinks' original. Ray Davies still regards it as the group's finest single, and he may well be right. It was unfortunate not to emulate the chart position of 'You Really Got Me', but met tough competition from The Supremes' 'Baby Love' and The Rolling Stones' 'Little Red Rooster'.

The B-side was typical Kinks' R&B of the period with a lyric crying out for a personal need to change and keep moving in an age when modernity ruled.

TIRED OF WAITING FOR YOU/COME ON NOW

RELEASED: JANUARY 1965
ORIGINAL UK ISSUE: PYE 7N 15759

Although recorded at the same session as 'All Day And All Of The Night', the Kinks' third A-side was a striking departure. This time around there was no frantic guitar solo from Dave, but a steady riff which highlighted the insistent, almost hypnotic, repetition of the song title. The narrator's neurotic fixation on his lover's tardiness seemed a strange subject for a pop song but typical of Davies who always liked to warp a love ballad in order to provide a more acute emotional response. Although 'Tired Of Waiting' sold 50,000 less copies than 'All Day And All Of The Night', it provided their all-important second UK chart topper and established them as Britain's third most successful group, behind the Beatles and the Stones. It was also their third consecutive Top 10 hit in America. The group were undertaking a world tour when Ray learned all this good news. "One of the happiest times I had was in Singapore when 'Tired Of Waiting For You' got to number 1," he remembered. "We'd been on a world tour and I was really homesick being on the road. And the *Daily Mirror* or one of those papers phoned me up to tell me the record was number 1 in England. I was really lonely. So I got a bottle of champagne and I got the waiter who brought it in, who couldn't speak English, to have a drink with me. That was one of the happiest times. Just that moment."

The B-side of the single, 'Come On Now' was also impressive and like 'Tired Of Waiting For You' was featured on the group's first album. Ray's wife Rasa can be heard on this flip side and she would later appear on a number of A-sides throughout the Pye era.

EV'RYBODY'S GONNA BE HAPPY/WHO'LL BE THE NEXT IN LINE

RELEASED: MARCH 1965
ORIGINAL UK ISSUE: PYE 7N 15813

The momentum that the Kinks had built up over the previous eight months was derailed by this desultory release, which barely scraped into the UK Top 20 and failed to sell even a quarter of the number of copies of 'Tired Of Waiting For You' in the British market. Although the performance was exuberant enough, the take-it-or-leave-it riff, muted clapping, lack of a memorable hook and generally ramshackle approach all contributed to its chart failure. "That wasn't written as a single," Ray pleaded, but he was the one who was pushing for its release against the better judgement of producer Shel Talmy. "I wanted to experiment with rhythms," Davies explained in mitigation. "We were on tour with the Motown band, Earl Van Dyke's band, and we were exposed to their sort of punching rhythm. There were no home studios in those days, so we had to come up with a master in a three-hour session. In effect, the single was the demo of the song."

The Kinks' American record company, Reprise, recognized the commercial limitations of 'Ev'rybody's Gonna Be Happy', so delayed its release and subsequently elevated its B-side as the main track. 'Who'll Be The Next In Line' featured a world-weary vocal from Ray and a vindictive lyric. However, it was clearly not good single material and failed to register in the US Top 40. That said, both sides were superior to virtually all the material on the group's second album, which was issued a couple of months before.

SET ME FREE/I NEED YOU

RELEASED: MAY 1965
ORIGINAL UK ISSUE: PYE 7N 15854

The need to return with a classy single prompted Ray to provide one of the best vocal performances of his career. Reminiscent of 'Tired Of Waiting', the track continued a trend to alternate single releases between slow-paced numbers and fast rockers. Although this single did not challenge for number 1, it succeeded in returning the group to the UK Top 10.

The B-side recalled the insistence of 'You Really Got Me' and was based around a similar riff. Davies betrays the same intense urgency here as he did in the lyrics to 'All Day And All Of The Night'.

SEE MY FRIEND/NEVER MET A GIRL LIKE YOU BEFORE
RELEASED: JULY 1965
ORIGINAL UK ISSUE: PYE 7N 15919

One of the most innovative and adventurous singles in the Kinks' canon, this was probably the earliest known example of what became known as "raga rock" – the fusion of Eastern and Western musical influences. The sitar-like sound featured on the disc pre-empted such raga classics as the Beatles' 'Norwegian Wood', the Byrds' 'Why', the Yardbirds' 'Shapes Of Things' and the Rolling Stones' 'Paint It Black'. In common with the Byrds and the Stones, the Kinks achieved the effects without actually using a sitar. While recording, Ray held his 12-string Framus guitar very close to the microphone resulting in slight feedback. Producer Shel Talmy then extended the drone through double tracking and compression and Dave duplicated the effect on his electric guitar. The unusual sound was complemented by a haunting vocal from Ray, which echoed the guitar drone.

Appropriately, the musical and vocal inspiration came from India. During their recent world tour, Davies had spent time near the Indian Ocean, where he heard fishermen chanting in unison. His attempt to duplicate those strange harmonies in his imagination brought an eerie feel to the finished recording. If the instrumentation and vocals sounded unique, then the lyrics were no less innovative. At a time when sexually explicit lyrics were anathema to mainstream pop pundits, Davies dared write a composition with strong overtones of homosexuality in the story of a jilted lover forced to seek alternate companionship "across the river". There was enough uncertainty about the subject matter to save Davies from a radio ban and Pye quickly modified the song title on subsequent pressings to the plural 'See My Friends' to avoid censure. In most interviews, Davies was suitably vague about his theme and the majority of pop journalists would never have mentioned the ultimate taboo of homosexuality in print. Fleet Street was different, however, and Davies risked his arm by revealing categorically to Maureen Cleave the true nature of the composition. "The song is about homosexuality," he stated. "I know a person in this business who is quite normal and good looking, but girls have given him such a rotten deal that he becomes a sort of queer. He has always got his friends. I mean it's like football teams and the way they're always kissing each other. Same sort of thing."

The B-side was a playful beat ballad, which opened with a teasing refrain from 'Tired Of Waiting For You' before

metamorphosing into a fast-paced rant.

TILL THE END OF THE DAY/WHERE HAVE ALL THE GOOD TIMES GONE?
RELEASED: NOVEMBER 1965
ORIGINAL UK ISSUE: PYE 7N 15981

After a surprisingly long gap of nearly four months, the Kinks bounced back with a song that recalled their previous hits, 'You Really Got Me' and 'All Day And All Of The Night'. The raucous vocal and guitar work were much welcomed by die-hard fans of the "old Kinks sound" and this was reflected in the sales. Although the disc failed to reach the Top 5, it remained in the charts for three months and sold more copies than any Kinks' recording since 'Tired Of Waiting For You'. The unfettered sound was partly inspired by Dave Davies's love of spontaneity. As he explained: "On our first trip to America, I was really influenced by all the guitar players I saw and heard there, particularly James Burton, who was playing in the house band on *Shindig*. That left its mark on my playing. I found it boring to practise, so I'd usually play it straight off the cuff. That's the way it worked best." On this session, drummer Clem Cattini deputized for Mick Avory.

The B-side, a barbed attack on the cult of youth prevalent in Sixties' popular culture, was taken from the group's disappointing second album, *Kinda Kinks*. An excellent song in its own right, it was later recorded by David Bowie on his 1973 covers album *Pin Ups*. That same year, Pye attempted to take advantage of the song's renewed profile by issuing the song as an A-side in its own right, but chart success proved elusive.

DEDICATED FOLLOWER OF FASHION/SITTIN' ON MY SOFA

RELEASED: FEBRUARY 1966

ORIGINAL UK ISSUE: PYE 7N 17064

Swinging London was at its zenith in 1966 when the Kinks poured light scorn on the excesses of the Carnaby Street shopaholic elite. Part novelty and part satire, the song was irresistible and

Ray's overtly camp vocal endeared him to the closet gays in the Kinks' circle. Unlike the subtle and disquieting 'See My Friend', 'Dedicated Follower Of Fashion' was comic homosexuality, as palatable to a family audience as Julian and Sandy in *Round The Horne*. Interestingly, Davies recalls the inspiration for this composition emerging from one of his darker moments. "That song came about after I'd had a violent punch-up at a party," he noted. "All these awful Sixties trendsetters would come around and wear the latest fashions and I would have on a pullover... Anyway, it was an appalling party and these people were making snide remarks about me, so I had a punch-up with a fashion designer. I said, 'All right, I'm gonna write a song about him, the dedicated follower of fashion'."

The single climbed to number 4 in the UK, their best chart-placing since 'Tired Of Waiting For You', although it actually sold 50,000 less copies than 'Till The End Of The Day'. The B-side, 'Sittin' On My Sofa' did not appear on any of their formal album releases but was later included on a cheapo sampler *Sunny Afternoon,* issued on Pye's budget label Marble Arch. It was another intriguing flip, marked by some jagged guitar work, predating Jimi Hendrix by a full year.

SUNNY AFTERNOON/I'M NOT LIKE EVERYBODY ELSE

RELEASED: JUNE 1966
ORIGINAL UK ISSUE: PYE 7N 17125

Instantly recognizable as the sound of the summer of '66, this not only restored the Kinks to number 1, but had the distinction of dislodging the Beatles' 'Paperback Writer' from the top spot. The single sold in excess of 300,000 copies placing it in a sales league last enjoyed by the Kinks during the heyday of 'You Really Got Me' and 'All Day And All Of The Night.' Unlike many of their singles from the mid-Sixties, 'Sunny Afternoon' was included on album (see *Face To Face*). Like the majority of Davies's best songs, it functioned on two levels as a work of satire and comedy. Beneath the languid vocal

there was much dark ennui to savour as Ray continued his fascinating observations on class-obsessed Britain. Those oblivious to such intricacies could still enjoy the number as an easy-going summer hit, summed up in the easily remembered chorus, "lazing on a sunny afternoon, in the summertime".

The B-side was arguably the finest of the group's career and another track that failed to find its way on to an official album. As a statement of intent, this could serve as Ray Davies's title tune. That it was sung by Dave made it appropriate to both brothers. After a dramatic guitar opening, the song builds in intensity, moving inexorably towards a screaming crescendo. A year earlier, this would have been called a protest song, but its cry for individual freedom is so shrill and the musical execution so raw that it transcends its time. It is almost an overlooked precursor of punk rock.

DEAD END STREET/ BIG BLACK SMOKE

RELEASED: NOVEMBER 1966

ORIGINAL UK ISSUE: PYE 7N 17222

A dour, funeral trombone opening sets the scene for this wilfully bleak song of urban depression. Having recently drawn material from observing the shenanigans of the middle and upper classes, Davies turns his eye towards the working classes with a domestic scenario redolent of post-war rationing or Victorian disregard. The inspiration for the song appears to have been manifold: the original idea was sparked by a book Ray read about the Depression in America during the Thirties. Other influences included his Lithuanian in-laws, whose plight as refugees sounded almost as sad as Eddie Kassner's harrowing stories of trying to make a living after the physical and psychological nightmare of living in a concentration camp. No doubt, the austerity of the Davies's home life during the Fifties provided further detail and the paintings of Hogarth conjured a visual representation of deprivation and hopelessness in an age long gone, but not forgotten. Ultimately, 'Dead End Street' was a kitchen sink drama without the drama – a static vision of working class stoicism and the all the more moving as a result.

The excellent B-side 'Big Black Smoke' was also redolent of another age with its anachronistic title, peeling bells and town crier cries of "oh yea". There was a touch of Thomas Hardy in the moral fable of a village girl seduced by dreams of city romance and the entire effect was like watching scenes from two different centuries – the bad Victorian girl and the Sixties runaway united in one song. It was as if Davies was commenting on the timeless theme of innocence corrupted.

WATERLOO SUNSET/ACT NICE AND GENTLE

RELEASED: MAY 1967
ORIGINAL UK ISSUE: PYE 7N 17314

Nearly six months passed before the Kinks returned with their next single — but it was worth the wait. Easily the best of Davies's London songs, this enshrined the unromantic Waterloo Bridge as an unlikely haven of romance. Originally, he had intended to write a song tentatively titled 'Liverpool Sunset', a pointed observation on the twilight of the beat boom, which had rendered redundant most of the Merseybeat acts who played the circuit when the Kinks first rose to fame. By chance, the Beatles chose that very moment to release their own odes to Liverpool with the brilliant double A-side 'Penny Lane'/'Strawberry Fields Forever'. This alone persuaded Ray to switch the geographical location and theme of his composition. Having determined to write about a London place name, he focused on Waterloo,

a station and bridge that brought back fond memories of his student days. Explaining the revisions that the song underwent, Davies revealed: "It happens a lot with my numbers. I work on a theme only to find as it nears completion someone else has come up with exactly the same melodic or lyrical idea. I suppose 'Waterloo' has stuck in my mind because I used to walk over Waterloo Bridge several nights a week on the way to art school when I was young... I've had the actual melody line in my mind for two or three years. If you look at the song as a kind of film I suppose 'Terry' would be Terence Stamp and 'Julie' would be Julie Christie. I've never really thought about the lyrics being sarcastic, but I suppose they are — it's just the way I feel."

Debate still rages among commentators regarding the names Terry and Julie. In his fictional autobiography, X-Ray, Davies suggests vaguely that he might have been thinking about his nephew Terry and an old flame immortalised under the name Julie Finkle. However, it is worth noting that the film *Far From The Madding Crowd*, starring Terence Stamp and Julie Christie, was popular at the time when Ray wrote the song. It is likely that both versions of the origins of the name are valid.

'Act Nice And Gentle,' the B-side of 'Waterloo Sunset', was not one of the Kinks' best. Both its title and country tinge were strongly reminiscent of the Beatles' 'Act Naturally', although the song could be said to have anticipated the later *Muswell Hillbillies*,

---

AUTUMN ALMANAC/ MISTER PLEASANT

RELEASED: OCTOBER 1967

ORIGINAL UK ISSUE: PYE 7N 17400

The gap between Kinks' singles continued to widen during the latter part of the Sixties, not least because Dave Davies was now issuing singles under his own name having enjoyed a massive summer hit with 'Death Of A Clown'. The Kinks' release schedule continued with this wistful seasonal tribute which kept the group in the UK Top 5. It was probably too light to challenge for number 1, but remains a much-loved and evocative portrayal of the Davies's early life in Muswell Hill, resplendent with images of bank holidays in Blackpool, roast beef Sunday dinners and football matches on a Saturday afternoon. Assuming Ray was still attending soccer games during this period, he must have been amused when the song was adopted as a football chant – "Arsenal are gonna crack, it's all part of the Everton attack".

The B-side, 'Mister Pleasant' had been slated as a potential single earlier in the year, only to be replaced by 'Waterloo Sunset'. With its bar room piano and music hall influences, the mood of the piece is light and upbeat, but there is a cruel tone of sarcasm in the lyrics and some sting-in-the-tail pathos when Mr Pleasant is finally cuckolded. The track was issued as a single on the Continent.

WONDERBOY/POLLY
RELEASED: APRIL 1968
ORIGINAL UK ISSUE: PYE 7N 17468

By 1968, the Kinks could look back proudly on 12 consecutive UK Top 20 hits, 11 of them in the Top 10 and the last five in the Top 5. And then there was the superficial 'Wonderboy'. Although it would have made a reasonable album track, the song lacked the charm or power of their recent work and was clearly too weak a single to make any impact. It charted for one week in the *NME* at number 28 and was as low as number 36 in other charts. For a group on such a roll, this was nothing short of a disaster. By comparison, even 'Ev'rybody's Gonna Be Happy' had been a stunning success. Despite strong advertising, 'Wonderboy' sold a shocking 27,000 copies, a mere tenth of that achieved by the preceding 'Autumn Almanac'.

The B-side was written about Polly Garter, the loose woman and earth mother featured in Dylan Thomas's play for voices *Under Milkwood*. Davies had intended to write a suite of songs inspired by the play, and this composition was faithful in its characterization of Polly. Alas, plans for a full-scale musical adaptation were shelved, although the idea carried over into *The Village Green Preservation Society*.

DAYS/SHE'S GOT EVERYTHING
RELEASED: JUNE 1968
ORIGINAL UK ISSUE: PYE 7N 17573

The Kinks arrested their fall from chart grace with this mid-paced offering which peaked at number 14. A beautiful lilt, with pensive lyrics that find strength and meaning in re-examining a dead relationship, the song contrasted markedly with Davies's recent, more humorous compositions. The track was later covered successfully by Kirsty MacColl.

The B-side was a surprise return to the old Kinks' sound, with a strong riff and hard-edged harmonies. What nobody knew at the time was that the track actually dated from the spring of 1966.

PLASTIC MAN/KING KONG
RELEASED: MARCH 1969

ORIGINAL UK ISSUE: PYE 7N 17724

After a gap of nine months, the longest wait yet for new single product, the Kinks returned with one of their least convincing offerings to date. It sounded an unashamed novelty and the satire was too obvious, too staid. The tune was jaunty but ephemeral and the lyrics banal to the point of infantile. Amusingly, the BBC felt obliged to ban the song due to Ray's saucy phrase "plastic bum". Like 'Wonderboy', it peaked at number 28 in the *NME*, selling a paltry 27,000 copies along the way.

The B-side was an odd song in the group's canon. The production was very subdued with the Kinks often sounding buried in a most peculiar mix. Stranger still, Ray's warbling vocal bore an uncanny resemblance to that of Marc Bolan.

DRIVIN'/MINDLESS CHILD OF MOTHERHOOD
RELEASED: JUNE 1969

ORIGINAL UK ISSUE: PYE 7N 17776

Although reasonably commercial, this was the single which heralded the unthinkable – the first Kinks' record since their chart debut to fail to reach the *NME* Top 30. What had once seemed effortless was now a despairing struggle. This was the first of two pilot singles for their much-vaunted concept album *Arthur* and its failure did not auger well. The B-side was credited to "the Kinks featuring Dave Davies". It kept alive forlorn hopes of a possible solo album from the younger brother.

SHANGRI-LA/THIS MAN HE WEEPS TONIGHT
RELEASED: SEPTEMBER 1969

ORIGINAL UK ISSUE: PYE 7N 17812

The undisputed showcase of the forthcoming *Arthur*, this was the song that would surely restore the Kinks' chart glories big time. As moving and ambitious a record as the group had ever recorded, it had a mock epic grandeur and bristled with intelligent lyrics that mixed pathos and social awareness in devastating fashion. For all that, it failed – miserably and unconditionally. Not only did it fall outside the all-important *NME* Top 30, but failed even to register in the *Record Retailer* Top 50. What probably killed the record was its audacity and length. Although the Beatles could break the seven-minute barrier with 'Hey Jude', radio programmers were not likely to allow the five-and-a-half minute 'Shangri-la' the same luxury.

As recent tradition dictated, the B-side was a Dave Davies composition that sounded suspiciously like a solo outing. Although fairly good, the vocal was again mixed surprisingly low, except in the upbeat chorus.

VICTORIA/
MR CHURCHILL SAYS
RELEASED: DECEMBER 1969
ORIGINAL UK ISSUE: PYE 7N 17865

The third single from *Arthur*, this was released after the album but proved

commercial enough to creep into the *NME* chart for one week at number 30. Sales patterns were the same as 'Wonderboy' and 'Plastic Man'. 'Victoria' boasted a good hook line and strong vocals, but was not quite up to the group's best. The track was later improbably covered by the Fall who enjoyed approximately the same chart position a full 18 years later.

The lacklustre B-side sounded no better removed from its context as part of *Arthur*. This was the first single on which the Kinks featured two previously released album tracks. In the US, where 'Drivin' was issued two months prior to its UK appearance, the flip side was another album track, 'Brainwashed'.

LOLA /BERKELEY MEWS
RELEASED: JUNE 1970
ORIGINAL UK ISSUE: PYE 7N 17961

Just when the Kinks' singles career had seemed at an inglorious end, they unexpectedly bounced back with a song which would rank alongside their most famous. On 1 August 1970, it dislodged

Free's 'All Right Now' from the top of the *NME* charts and also reached number 9 in the US, their first Stateside hit since 'Sunny Afternoon' four years before. The song's risqué nature prompted a radio ban in Australia, but its camp appeal was deemed acceptable by the BBC, although they did force Davies to insert the word "cherry cola" in place of "Coca Cola" on the UK single version of the track. When the group played the song on *Top Of The Pops*, Ray remembers a cameraman blowing kisses at him. "The song is actually meant to show that things aren't always what they seem," he reasoned at the time. "In such realms, you could think one thing and something else would be hidden, lurking in the shadow. I like writing songs with stories about people. I live in a strange world to some, but I think the world is a lot stranger. ...if you read into the lyric, you'll see the song is only about friendship."

The peculiar B-side, 'Berkeley Mews', was a playful novelty number with pub piano and an almost drunken vocal revel. There were also some strong musical influences from the Forties amid the chaotic arrangement.

APEMAN/RATS
RELEASED: NOVEMBER 1970
ORIGINAL UK ISSUE: PYE 7N 45016

The Kinks concluded their career at Pye with a welcome Top 5 hit and their last ever appearance in the Top 10. This was a pleasing novelty number in most respects and a baptism of embarrassment for new boy John Gosling who made his television debut on *Top Of The Pops* dressed as a gorilla. Having previously had to change a single word on 'Lola' from "Coca" to "cherry" for the BBC, Davies was obliged to do the same here for American radio which insisted that the word "foggin'" required clearer enunciation.

The B-side was a hard-rocking Dave Davies number which, like 'Apeman', was included on their concomitant album, *The Kinks Part One – Lola Versus Powerman And The Moneygoround.*

E.P.S

KINKSIZE SESSION
RELEASED: NOVEMBER 1964
ORIGINAL UK ISSUE: PYE NEP 24200

Issued just in time for the Christmas market, this EP featured four tracks unavailable on contemporaneous albums or B-sides. The opening track was Richard Berry's 'Louie Louie', a song whose seminal riff has often been claimed as the template for much of the Kinks' early work. There was also a chance to hear 'I've Got That Feeling', previously issued as a cover by one of Larry Page's protégés, the Orchids.

Full track listing: Louie Louie; I Gotta Go Now; Things Are Getting Better; I've Got That Feeling.

KINKSIZE HITS
RELEASED: JANUARY 1965
ORIGINAL UK ISSUE: PYE NEP 24203

This featured the A and B-sides of the group's hit singles 'You Really Got Me' and 'All Day Of The Night' and was released on the same day as 'Tired Of Waiting For You'.

Full track listing: You Really Got Me; It's Alright; All Day And All Of The Night; I Gotta Move.

KWYET KINKS
RELEASED: SEPTEMBER 1965
ORIGINAL UK ISSUE: PYE NEP 24221

Another work of entirely new material, this was the group's most popular excursion into the EP market, largely thanks to the presence of the scintillating 'A Well Respected Man'. It was undoubtedly one of the most articulate compositions written by a pop group up until that time. The song represented a crucial new phase in Davies's songwriting with its playful satire of the aspiring middle classes. Later, Davies would construct entire albums around this theme, but seldom captured the sardonic spontaneity evident here. Pye's decision to relegate the song to an EP rather issuing the track as a single was a major blunder for it was clearly one of the most commercial tracks recorded by the group. A probable candidate for number 1, it was played frequently on radio and paved the way for songs like 'Dedicated Follower Of Fashion'. The Kinks' US record company Reprise, which had no EP outlet, promptly released 'A Well Respected Man' as a single. Despite the group's non-availability for promotion, the song climbed to an impressive number 13 in the Hot 100. The remainder of this EP was understandably eclipsed by its most famous track, but deserves attention. Significantly, the material herein was far superior to most of the songs included on Kinks' albums of the time.

'Wait Till The Summer Comes Along' (erroneously credited to Ray Davies) was a Dave Davies Dylanesque ballad with a slight country tinge. 'Such A Shame' revealed the group caught between the beat and folk rock traditions, while the concluding 'Don't You Fret' featured a suitably dramatic guitar crescendo set against Ray's conciliatory lyrics.

Full track listing: Wait Till The Summer Comes Along; Such A Shame; A Well Respected Man; Don't You Fret.

DEDICATED KINKS
RELEASED: JULY 1966
ORIGINAL UK ISSUE: PYE NEP 24258

Several experimental EPs of new Kinks' material were planned around this period, then cancelled. Instead, Pye elected to recycle older material, this time combining four previous Kinks' A-sides.

Full track listing: Dedicated Follower Of Fashion; Till The End Of The Day; See My Friend; Set Me Free.

THE KINKS
RELEASED: APRIL 1968
ORIGINAL UK ISSUE: PYE NEP 24296

Four tracks were plucked from the recently released *Something Else By The Kinks* for this 1968 EP. Interestingly, this was issued on the same day as the rival *Dave Davies Hits*, which featured 'Death Of A Clown', 'Love Me Till The Sun Shines', 'Funny Face' and 'Susannah's Still Alive'.

Full track listing: David Watts; Two Sisters; Lazy Old Sun; Situation Vacant.

THE KINKS (PERCY)
RELEASED: APRIL 1971
ORIGINAL UK ISSUE: PYE 7NX 8001

This was a selection of the best songs from the *Percy* soundtrack, bypassing the instrumentals therein. An excellent, value for money release on 33 rpm.

Full track listing: God's Children; The Way Love Used To Be; Moments; Dreams.

THE KINKS – MINI MONSTERS
RELEASED: AUGUST 1971
ORIGINAL UK ISSUE: PYE PMM 100

Released at the end of the EP age, this was nothing more than a cash-in with no redeeming value. The track selection was logically and aesthetically inexplicable.

Full track listing: You Really Got Me; Set Me Free; Wonderboy; Long Tall Shorty.

Following the termination of the Kinks' contract with Pye, the company released several more EPs in the post-punk era, all featuring previously issued material: *Big Deal* (1977), *Yesteryear* (1978) and *The Kinks – Flashback* (1980). PRT, which inherited the Pye catalogue, followed suit with *You Really Got Me* (1983). None of these are worthy of more than cursory consideration.

THE KINKS LIVE EP
RELEASED: JULY 1980
ORIGINAL UK ISSUE: ARISTA ARIST 360

Arista Records unexpectedly entered the EP market with this selection of tracks borrowed from the double live album *One For The Road*.

Full track listing: David Watts; Where Have All The Good Times Gone?; Attitude; Victoria.

BETTER THINGS
RELEASED: JUNE 1981
ORIGINAL UK ISSUE: ARISTA ARIST 415/KINKS 1

Released a month before the single 'Better Days', this featured two tracks from *One For The Road* and an alternate take of 'Massive Reductions'.

Full track listing: Better Things; Massive Reduction(s); Lola; David Watts.

STATE OF CONFUSION
RELEASED: MARCH 1984
ORIGINAL UK ISSUE ARISTA ARIST 560

This strange EP was a largely pointless selection of two cuts from *State Of Confusion* and *One For The Road*, respectively.

Full track listing: State Of Confusion; Heart Of Gold; Lola; 20th Century Man.

DID YA
RELEASED: OCTOBER 1991
ORIGINAL ISSUE: COLUMBIA 44 K 74050
(US ONLY)

The CD equivalent of an EP, this unusual release combined the single 'Did Ya' with a live version of 'I Gotta Move' and a re-recording of 'Days', which had gained prominence as a hit for Kirsty MacColl two years previously. Completing this interesting selection were two otherwise unissued songs: 'New World' and Dave Davies's 'Look Through Any Doorway'.

Full track listing: Did Ya; I Gotta Move; Days; New World; Look Through Any Doorway.

WATERLOO SUNSET '94

RELEASED: OCTOBER 1994

ORIGINAL UK ISSUE: KONK/GRAPEVINE KNKCD 2

This CD release was issued during the same month as the first issue of *To The Bone* and featured two selections from that album, plus the previously unissued 'Elevator Man' and 'On The Outside'.

Full track listing: Waterloo Sunset; You Really Got Me; Elevator Man; On The Outside.

THE DAYS EP

RELEASED: JANUARY 1997

ORIGINAL UK ISSUE: WHEN WEN X 1016

Subtitled *30 Years Of Yellow Pages 1966-1996*, this CD EP was inspired by the *Yellow Pages* television advertisement featuring 'Days'. All tracks were previously issued items.

Full track listing: Days; You Really Got Me; Dead End Street; Lola.

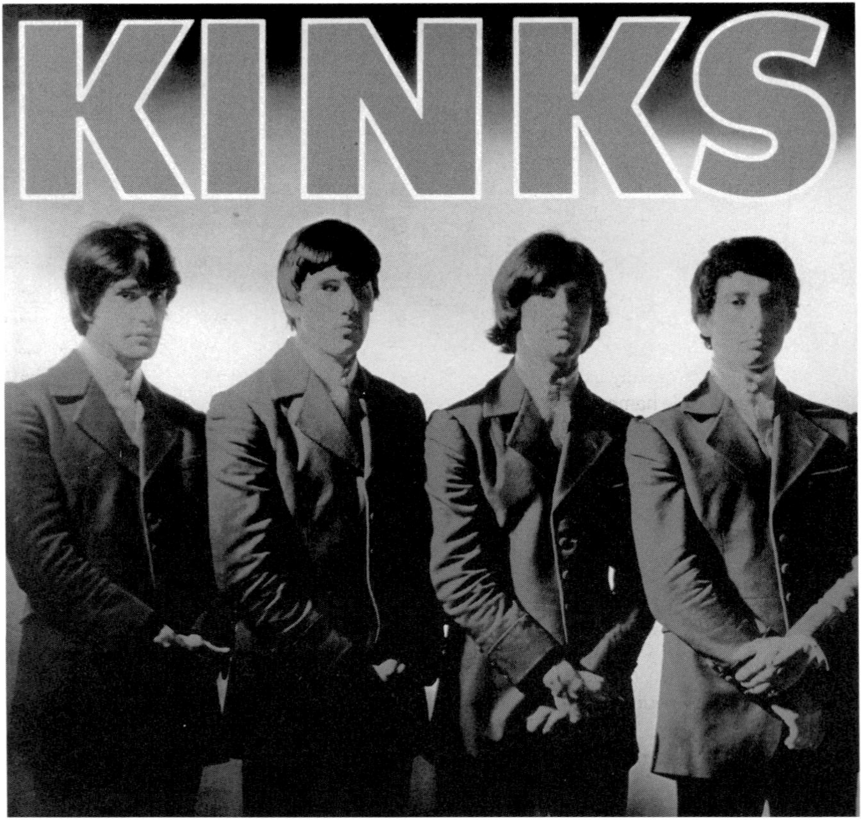
KINKS

ALBUMS
KINKS

RELEASED: OCTOBER 1964

ORIGINAL UK ISSUE: PYE NPL 18096 (MONO); NSPL 83021 (STEREO)

With their third single, 'You Really Got Me', heading for number 1, the Kinks were herded into the studio to complete an album to cash in on the Christmas market. "We had a week to do it," Dave Davies remembered. "I don't know how we managed. There were only about six original songs on that LP because of the time, and the rest were things we knew and could do very quickly in the time. As I remember, the last sessions for that album, there were actually people hammering on the door to get in because we were running a bit over time."

The Kinks' debut album was certainly no classic, although it was no worse and arguably considerably better than the work of many of their pop contemporaries. Ironically, Davies remembers taking the Beatles as a role model in deciding to mix group originals with cover material. Alas, *Kinks* was no match for *Beatles For Sale*, nor even *Please Please Me*, which had been recorded on a similarly tight schedule. Without the benefit of a spell in Hamburg, the Kinks were forced to rely on material borrowed from their current live set. They were still an impressionable group coming to terms with performances at larger venues and over-reliant on familiar R&B standards. What this album captured was their early exuberance and, if nothing else, it serves as a reminder of the inchoate charm and general tightness of their concerts, which were already serving as a talking point among the pop elite.

BEAUTIFUL DELILAH

The album opens with a fast version of this Chuck Berry classic, with Ray and Dave both featured on vocals. A solid R&B effort, it reveals how well rehearsed the group was when they entered the studio for their first LP. Unrestrained and at times primitive, such songs displayed the essence of the Kinks' roots during a period when they were still formulating their own sound.

SO MYSTIFYING

With a strong tambourine backing and some distinctly American phrasing from Ray, this was a half decent song, with a hint of the Stones. Dave's voice is also noticeable in the mix, a firm indication of a greater democracy in the distribution of vocal credits during the early period.

JUST CAN'T GO TO SLEEP

Ray Davies often suffered from insomnia and his sleepless nights inspired a song as early as this first album. The Beatles' influence, vocally and instrumentally, is evident here, mutated through the earlier girl group sound.

LONG TALL SHORTY

This raucous version of Don Covay's much covered R&B standard was a real showcase for Dave Davies, who handles the vocal line with considerable aplomb. Again, it provides an intriguing insight into the group's live repertoire of the period.

I TOOK MY BABY HOME

American R&B influences continued to dominate the album with this solid work-out, with both drums and harmonica the dominating instruments.

I'M A LOVER NOT A FIGHTER

The sceptre of the Rolling Stones, then Britain's number 2 group, hovered over parts of the album, as this track testifies. Dave Davies is let loose for some raspy-voiced screeching and a smart lead guitar break, backed by exuberant clapping. As a period piece, it works reasonably well.

YOU REALLY GOT ME

The quintessential sound of the Kinks and their first number 1 hit is modestly placed at the end of the album's first side. Listening to the track in the context of the LP reveals the way in which the Kinks were moving away from their imitative R&B sound towards a harder-edged, riff-based pop. Manager Larry Page later said that he built the act around the sound of the Kingsmen, whose seminal 'Louie Louie' was released that same year. However, Dave Davies recalls the origins of that guitar sound in a film of the Montreux Jazz Festival in which Jimmy Guiffre and Gerry Mulligan played 'Train On The River'. Ray Davies, for his part, remembers composing the song on a piano in his parents' front room. From these disparate influences came a track which kick-started the Kinks' career and provided a template for all their riff-based rock songs hereafter.

CADILLAC

The Bo Diddley sound influenced all of the Kinks' R&B/pop contemporaries, including the Rolling Stones, the Animals, the Pretty Things and the Yardbirds. Here, the familiar Diddley shuffle, with prominent harmonica and bass work, is played out for the umpteenth time on what was another live favourite and often the opening number to the Kinks' set.

BALD HEADED WOMAN

The ever astute producer Shel Talmy bagged a songwriting credit on this crude reworking of a public domain song. "For a first album, I thought it would be a good idea to do some non-original stuff," he told me. "On one hit song Ray was hardly established as the great songwriter." With prominent music publishers in their circle, it was regrettable that the Kinks agreed to record what was little more than a riff and a couple of verses of frankly appalling material. In a vain attempt to improve the song, Jimmy Page was employed as session guitarist.

REVENGE

This instrumental was first attempted when the Kinks were still known as the Ravens. Uniquely credited to Ray Davies and manager Larry Page, it was an early attempt to establish a distinctive sound. "I sat down with Ray and told him that the one thing that would sell records would be riffs," Page remembers. "Just riffs going all the way through." Interestingly, this was briefly used as the opening theme to television's *Ready Steady Go!*

TOO MUCH MONKEY BUSINESS

Like the Stones, the Kinks were enamoured of Chuck Berry and this was the second of his compositions to appear on the album. Although not in the same class as the best white pop R&B of the period, it was a passable attempt.

I'VE BEEN DRIVING ON BALD MOUNTAIN

Remarkably, Talmy's second adapted composition on the album was even worse than the previous one. Given the time constraints, the Kinks seemed content to allow this below par number to be included without complaint. "Nobody disagreed with the material," Talmy points out. "There were no great traumas – nothing like that."

STOP YOUR SOBBING

After all the R&B-related tunes, it was a pleasant surprise to hear an undiluted pop outing. Ray Davies's fragile vocal works well on this polite protest against a girlfriend's excess of emotion. The singer sounds irrationally irked by the girl's sobbing in the same neurotic way that he would later damn unpunctuality in 'Tired Of Waiting For You'. Mid-way through the song, he admonishes the lachrymose lady with the plea "Stop it!" in a tone more in keeping with a command to a disobedient dog. Always a hidden gem in the Kinks' canon, this song was belatedly brought to the masses courtesy of the Pretenders' hit cover in 1979.

GOT LOVE IF YOU WANT IT

Concluding the album with this Slim Harpo number, the Kinks again elected to impress us with their R&B credentials. Although the vocal was slight and whiny and the rudimentary backing deceptively low key, the group let rip towards the end with an elongated harmonica break and some solid upfront drumming, presumably the work of Mick Avory.

KINDA KINKS

RELEASED: MARCH 1965

ORIGINAL UK ISSUE: PYE NPL 18112

The Kinks' second album was reputedly recorded within a matter of days, with all but two tracks completed at Pye Studios in mid-February, barely a month before its release. As the group had just returned from a world tour, they were in no condition to commence a new album immediately and the work sounds terribly rushed and unfocused. It is evident that Davies had no time to complete any decent new songs and those attempted here sound painfully like filler, spread over 27-and-a-half minutes. Of course, at a time when the focus was almost entirely on singles, a mediocre album like this was par for the course for most beat groups. No stereo release was sanctioned, as neither Pye nor the group felt it was worth the extra expense. That this work now stands as part of the Kinks' canon is no doubt a terrible embarrassment to Ray Davies, but it remains a revealing curio from a period when albums cashed in on singles without apology.

LOOK FOR ME BABY

Rudimentary R&B with the requisite Merseybeat leanings. Even for early 1965, the sound is thin to the point of minimalist. This was the type of number that the Kinks could play in their live set and was perfect for the package tour circuit.

GOT MY FEET ON THE GROUND

One of two tracks on the album recorded in December 1964, this derivative blues was a promising cameo for Dave Davies, who co-wrote the song with his brother. At this point, Dave was a major contributor to the group's albums and his vocal style was far more in keeping with the bluesier material, unlike the uncertain wailing of brother Ray.

NOTHIN' IN THIS WORLD CAN STOP ME WORRYIN' 'BOUT THAT GIRL

A strong blues/folk influence again permeates Davies's writing, this time set against an acoustic backing. The result is one of the more affective mood pieces on the album, although the composition is less than world-shattering.

NAGGIN'

Often referred to on albums as 'Naggin' Woman', this track exposed the limitations of Ray's whiny voice when applied to a blues workout. He is certainly no Eric Burdon or Van Morrison and the vocal might have been better handled by his brother. The recording sounds very much like an early demo and from the amateurish feel it is difficult to believe that they could have attempted more than a couple of takes.

WONDER WHERE MY BABY IS

This was much a much more commercial pop sound reminiscent of their singles repertoire. Typical B-side material, it fitted well on to the album and the insistent riff was notable.

TIRED OF WAITING FOR YOU

The general paucity of material on offer was emphasized by the inclusion of their current number 1 hit. It easily eclipses everything else on this record, displaying the power of the Kinks when they were given the opportunity to concentrate on a composition. Ray's world weary vocal, backed by strong harmonies, a gulping bass line and a catchy chorus, proved an irresistible combination. His abilities as a songwriter were emphasized by the daring use of such an anti-romantic theme. The almost neurotic emphasis on his lover's tardiness threatens the foundations of their relationship, a feeling which is rammed home by the ingenious play on the title phrase which is

repeated and elaborated upon: "So tired... tired of waiting... tired of waiting for you."

DANCING IN THE STREET

Ray goes Motown on a regrettably watered-down version of Martha & The Vandellas' contemporaneous hit. It's the familiar beat group by numbers version of black music, likeable in concert but mere padding when placed on an album. The Kinks had recently toured with the Tamla Motown group, which largely explains their decision to cover this track.

DON'T EVER CHANGE

Obviously inspired by the Drifters' 'Save The Last Dance For Me', this had all the passion of an amateur dramatic society player aping Ben E. King. At least the insecurity prevalent in the lyrical theme looked forward to more mature work.

COME ON NOW

When it came to R&B-inspired material, Dave Davies sounded far more confident and accomplished, a point underlined by

this track, which also served as a strong B-side to 'Tired Of Waiting For You'. The guitar riff is also strong and the song emerges as one of the highlights of a less than auspicious album.

SO LONG

Folk rock was starting to make its presence known in the pop world during early 1965 and the Kinks anticipated matters with this gentle acoustic ballad, complete with references to leaving "Muswell town". This was one of the earliest hints of Ray's troubled transition towards pop stardom as he says goodbye to home life, albeit without too much angst.

YOU SHOULDN'T BE SAD

This raucous number was most noticeable for the frantic vocals, which betray the influence of the Spector girl group sound. It's a bizarre pastiche from a group still experimenting with different influences as if uncertain about which direction their music is likely to take.

SOMETHING BETTER BEGINNING

The final track was the earliest recording on the album, having been cut in December 1964. Both the theme and melody are a little reminiscent of the Drifters' 'Save The Last Dance For Me'. A month after the release of the album, the chart-topping Honeycombs, another act on Pye, took the song to number 39 in the UK singles charts, partly confirming Ray Davies's early promise as a songwriter.

THE KINK KONTROVERSY

THE KINKS KONTROVERSY

RELEASED: NOVEMBER 1965

ORIGINAL UK ISSUE: PYE NP: 18131 (MONO); SSPL 18131 (STEREO)

Although a considerable improvement on *Kinda Kinks*, the group's third album was still a lacklustre affair, again completed within a week. Ray Davies took a much greater interest in promoting his songwriting, even though the results were decidedly erratic. At least the production and playing sounded a lot sharper in places, suggesting that the Kinks were adjusting to the speed of studio work, even though their material was erratic and often below par. Ultimately, the album was a transitional work, part of which looked back to their R&B roots, while other tracks indicated Davies's continued emergence as a songwriter of potentially exceptional talent. Although the cover artwork refers to the album as *The Kink Kontroversy* the original label clearly states *The Kinks Kontroversy*.

MILK COW BLUES

This John Estes R&B staple was a live favourite, always played with great enthusiasm. The production is much sharper than similar efforts on their previous album, while Dave Davies plays with great gusto on what was reputedly a one take song.

RING THE BELLS

Here was one of the first examples on album of Ray finding his voice on material with a distinctly ambiguous edge. Although ostensibly a song of elation, it is sung in such a languid, sanguine manner that the sentiments sound mournful. The ringing bells of the title would be more appropriate for a funeral than for a wedding. Easily overlooked, this was one of Ray's more affecting songs of the period.

GOTTA GET THE FIRST PLANE HOME

This was a fairly derivative R&B piece complete with a short harmonica break. The Stones' influence was still present, but by now the Kinks had their own distinctive style, with Ray's voice instantly recognizable.

WHEN I SEE THAT GIRL OF MINE

Another plodding arrangement that sounds suspiciously like filler. Here was a final glimpse of the old Merseybeat influences that characterized the group's early work.

I AM FREE

Dave Davies was living the life of a pop star with hedonistic glee at this time, but his bacchanalian excesses also resulted in some occasional dark nights of the soul. This song, although unremarkable, fitted in well with the other material on the album and kick-started Dave's song-writing, which would improve markedly later in the decade.

TILL THE END OF THE DAY

A perfect complement to the other material on the album, this instant hit recalled the primal sound of the Kinks' first two singles. Dave's playing is raw and loose while the backbeat and tambourine attract attention. In common with their previous two albums, the Kinks allowed their current hit single to be included, but studiously avoided adding other A-sides, even at a time when questions were being asked about Ray's songwriting output.

THE WORLD KEEPS GOING ROUND

With its neurotic, fatalistic lyrics, this was another typical Davies song of the time. Unfortunately, the melody and arrangement left much to be desired, despite the presence of ace session pianist Nicky Hopkins.

I'M ON AN ISLAND

Having toured the world, it was inevitable that Davies would pick up some musical ideas on his foreign travels.

This upbeat calypso number, with prominent piano, anticipated a more cosmopolitan style, which would reach fruition on their next album.

WHERE HAVE ALL THE GOOD TIMES GONE?

Undoubtedly one of the best songs on the album, this boasted a memorable melody and some impressive harmony vocals from the Davies brothers. Indeed, much of the album might have been improved by other unison vocals in this style. The lyrics were also revealing, indicating Ray Davies' restlessness and increasing cynicism. A mere two years into the pop game and he was already looking back with regret at a lost golden age, which probably never existed outside of his fertile imagination. "Everybody seemed to be having a good time," he recalled. "As a realist, I knew that the good times had to have a payback."

IT'S TOO LATE

With honky-tonk piano and a country style vocal, this was another departure, starting a trail that would end with the recording of *Muswell Hillbillies* five years later.

WHAT'S IN STORE FOR ME?

The sound of barrel-scraping should have accompanied this track, as it was one of Davies's least memorable tunes on the album. Like many other songs from this period, it lacked craft and gave the impression that Davies was writing to a formula.

YOU CAN'T WIN

The concluding track was a surprise success, with some assured playing from Dave. Talmy created an effective wall of sound in which the vocals and instruments coalesced. Although the track was not especially radical, the thrust of the piece was impressive and indicated what might have been achieved if more time had been spent on some of the lesser songs herein.

FACE TO FACE

RELEASED: OCTOBER 1966

ORIGINAL UK ISSUE: PYE NPL 18149 (MONO)/NPSL 18149 (STEREO)

The Kinks' first serious foray into the albums market was originally an even more ambitious work on which Ray Davies envisaged connecting tracks with various sound effects. Such a work would have predated the Beatles' groundbreaking *Sgt Pepper's Lonely Hearts Club Band* by the best part of a year, but in the end the concept was compromised and the idea of linking songs with sound montages largely abandoned. Nevertheless, this album represented a defining moment in the Kinks' career, with Davies emerging as one of the country's most important songwriters and for the first time providing us with a work that included no less than 14 of his compositions. Having previously recorded albums almost as an afterthought, the group was now ready to exploit the format as a major means of artistic expression.

PARTY LINE

The initial idea of using various sound effects was evident on this track, which opens with the sound of a ringing phone and the cultured tones of manager Grenville Collins asking, "Who's that speaking, please?" Dave sings lead and relates the humour, annoyance and practical difficulties of gaining access to your own phone when you choose to share a line. Rhythmically, the song betrayed a strong skiffle influence and an appropriate party atmosphere. There was even a sly hint of sexual ambiguity, pre-empting 'Lola', in the line, "Is she a she at all?"

ROSY, WON'T YOU PLEASE COME HOME

Ray Davies was deeply affected by his sister Rosy's decision to emigrate to Australia in November 1963. Here his suppressed feelings are translated into song and he does not even attempt to disguise the name of his sibling. One of the most poignant moments on the album, the song is given added depth by the presence of a harpsichord and the low vocal mix. Mid-way through the track, Davies manages to throw in some passing comments on class divisions and social mobility, which would be employed even more forcibly on several other tracks.

DANDY

An American hit for Herman's Hermits and covered in the UK by Clinton Ford, this sounded like the tale of a Rakish Edwardian cad, transposed to Swinging London. The strong music hall influence was evident throughout. Consciously or otherwise, the composition was most likely inspired by the contemporaneous film and song 'Alfie', which also dealt with promiscuity and bachelorhood. In the movie, the ageing protagonist is forced to face his decline as a Lothario, but in Davies's fictional universe, the Don Juan is ultimately celebrated rather than castigated.

TOO MUCH ON MY MIND

Reflective in tone, this mood piece was neatly complemented by the stately harpsichord. The title alone could serve as Ray Davies's theme song, with references to his insomnia and over-active brain. Viewed from a biographical point of view, the composition provided a revealing insight into Ray's troubled psyche during a period when he was beleaguered by publishing, management and record company disputes. As he pointed out at the time: "I worry about everything. One night I went round to Barry Fantoni's flat and then remembered that I'd left the tap dripping at home. It was on my mind all the time – in the end Barry had to run back to Muswell Hill so I could turn it off."

SESSION MAN

This satirical stab at a jobbing musician, who cares little whether he plays with rock musicians or orchestras, was incisive in its sarcasm. There was no hint of sympathy in the portrayal of this musical automaton, whose only aesthetic was union rules and payment by the hour. Given session man Nicky Hopkins' involvement throughout the album, it is difficult to believe that Ray wasn't making mischief.

RAINY DAY IN JUNE

Beginning with the sound effects of a storm, this was another fascinating track, which Ray later described as a fairy tale. Although he uses the storm in the sunshine as a metaphor for his own troubled career, the idea is underdeveloped lyrically. Nevertheless, the vocal is both impressive and affecting.

HOUSE IN THE COUNTRY

Taken at a faster pace, this was a sly dig at the process of embourgeiosement and a studied reflection on the *nouveau riche* with their fast cars and country homes. Of course, the irony is that the song emerged from Davies's own attempt to find a suitable suburban dwelling and it serves as an apposite comment on his own aspirations as a wealthy pop star. Kinks' fan Damon Albarn would later use the same theme and adapt the title for Blur's Oasis-baiting chart topper in 1995.

HOLIDAY IN WAIKIKI

In the mid-Sixties many visiting UK groups, including the Kinks, played in Waikiki. The experience inspired Ray to satirize the commercial exploitation evident on the island. He presents a wry tale of a person winning a trip to Hawaii in a newspaper competition, only to discover a cultural wasteland and phoney ethnicity, in which even the girls' grass skirts are made of PVC. In the background, Dave plays a disconcerting drone on his guitar for added effect.

MOST EXCLUSIVE RESIDENCE FOR SALE

A sister song to 'House In The Country', this satiric morality tale described the fall of an aristocrat through overspending on "girls and fancy jewellery". In the end, he is forced to sell his house in order to pay off his debts. The backing vocals are particularly notable, with the Kinks attempting to emulate the harmonies of the Beach Boys.

FANCY

Played on Ray's trusty Framus guitar, this was the most unusual song on the album. The insistent drone recalled the raga-styled 'See My Friend', while the lyrics were suitably enigmatic. At a time when external pressures were provoking questions about his ability to withstand the pressures of fame, Davies hid behind his seventh veil, announcing: "No one can penetrate me". There was also some sexual ambiguity at work in the title, with the listener never quite sure whether 'Fancy' is male or female.

LITTLE MISS QUEEN OF DARKNESS

This song featured the debut of bassist John Dalton, who was recruited after Pete Quaife was forced to retire from the group temporarily in the aftermath of a car crash. Prior to this album's release, it was announced that they were working on a song titled 'Girl Who Goes To Discotheques'. The composition evidently evolved into this track, which referred to the tribulations of a disco dancer. With Avory providing a decidedly military-style drum part and the band playing in an almost jug band style, the entire effect was merrily laid back. In many ways, this song was a lyrical precursor to 'Lola', complete with references to sexual uncertainty on the dance floor.

YOU'RE LOOKING FINE

The flow of the album was interrupted by this blues effort from Dave Davies. In some ways, it recalled the earlier R&B work of the group in 1964, but seemed out of context here.

SUNNY AFTERNOON

What could easily have been a poignant tale of the fall of an aristocrat backed by a suitably descending bass line is probably best remembered as a happy singalong by most listeners. The humorous references to the "big fat mama" underscored Davies's stoical reflections on high taxation. This was a period when the Labour Party had promised to tax the rich "until the pips squeak" and Ray, as a wealthy pop star, could easily imagine a scenario in which his earnings were decimated. While best remembered as a number 1 single in its own right, it should be noted how well the track fits onto this album, nestling comfortably alongside those other songs of *nouveau riche* overreaching and aristocratic debauchery – 'Most Exclusive Residence For Sale' and 'House In The Country'.

I'LL REMEMBER

The concluding track on the album was an interesting exercise in musical contrast with a fluttering piano set against the sharp, metallic guitar work of Dave Davies. Unusual in structure, it also featured a poignant lyric, with the protagonist squirreling away memories of the present in the firm knowledge that they would bring nostalgic reward in the future. An interesting conclusion to an often fascinating album.

SOMETHING ELSE BY THE KINKS

RELEASED: SEPTEMBER 1967

ORIGINAL UK ISSUE: PYE NPL 18193 (MONO)/NSPL 18193 (STEREO)

With Ray Davies entering his golden period as a songwriter, the Kinks unveiled one of their most impressive works. This album featured a stunning selection of themes and ideas from schoolboy nostalgia to nicotine addiction and sun worship. Musically, the work was no less eclectic, with flashes of psychedelia, hard rock, a sea shanty and even a touch of vaudeville. This may even have been the best collection of songs recorded by the group on one official album. What flaws that were evident seemed largely due to the sequencing of the tracks. For all its individual merits the album did not flow as well as it might. At times, the different styles clashed uneasily rather than complementing each other. What might have worked brilliantly as a suite of songs instead appeared strangely disparate in mood. However, such quibbles cannot disguise the merit and quality of the songs which should have pushed the group into a new league, critically and commercially. Regrettably, the album failed to sell in vast quantities. It remains a substantial and much underrated work outclassing even the excellent *Face To Face* .

DAVID WATTS

A scintillating opening track, this was one of the best Kinks' songs from this period – a strong melody, fascinating lyrics, a surging bass line and some neat harmonies. The sexual ambiguity implicit in the song came from two sources – part fictional and part autobiographical. Both Ray and Dave recall an old major named David Watts who booked them for a show in Rutland and later invited them to a party, which turned into an evening of saturnalian excess in which the younger brother was propositioned and bartered for as if he was the subject of an arranged marriage. In writing the song, however, Ray merely took the name David Watts as a tease, but retained the gay theme in his evocation of schoolboy hero worship. Here, Watts emerges as a Flashman character – a hunky sports hero, "gay and fancy free", but oblivious to the advances of girls. Amusingly, a touch of avarice enters the equation as the ever frugal Ray observes, "I wish all his money belonged to me". Fittingly, the song was later revived successfully to provide the Jam with a Top 30 hit.

DEATH OF A CLOWN

Co-written by Dave and Ray, this was the song that launched the younger brother's frustratingly undeveloped solo career. He could hardly have got off to a better start for this was a record easily the equal of the best Kinks' material of the period and wasn't far off reaching number 1. The plaintive piano opening, complete with some airy harmony work

by Ray's wife Rasa, set the scene for Dave's distinctly Dylanesque composition. The circus imagery was complemented by the musical backing and slightly hoarse vocal style as the symbolic death of a clown reflected a coming of age through marriage and the farewell of the infamous clubber Dave the Rave.

TWO SISTERS

With able assistance from Nicky Hopkins on harpsichord, plus a cello and viola backing, this was another of Davies's delicate domestic dramas reflecting on class distinctions and the contrasting rewards of singlehood and marriage. In expressing some of the kitchen sink imagery, Ray looked back to his childhood in North London. The song was also a transparent comment on the envy he felt for his brother who was clubbing most nights while Ray was coming to terms with marriage and parenthood. "It isn't just a feminine thing," Ray said of the song. "There were aspects of my relationship with my brother. That's the way I like to write… it's not good enough to write a song about a situation. I like to relate it to something else." Significantly, the composition ends on a conciliatory note, with the elder sister finding salvation in the joys of parenthood and losing her jealousy in an act of acceptance.

NO RETURN

Proof of the Kinks' stylistic diversity was evident on this surprise excursion into bossa nova/flamenco territory. Ray's falsetto is set against an arrangement, which conjures up images of Jose Feliciano and Antonio Carlos Jobim. This quiet reflection on a first love betrayed a light touch not dissimilar to Paul McCartney's minor pieces in the Beatles' canon.

HARRY RAG

This rumbustious recording sounded as though it had been borrowed from a sea shanty. A love song to nicotine addiction, it also revealed Davies's love of music hall with a rousing singalong chorus and some amusing reflections on the life of a stoical smoker.

TIN SOLDIER MAN

The kaleidoscopic shift of styles was further emphasized with this marching song, complete with a brass section. Lyrically, it seemed like a modern-day rewrite of 'The Grand Old Duke Of York'. Dave finds his place as a cheer leader in the background urging on the troops.

SITUATION VACANT

Another of Ray's mini-dramas, this was effectively a musical version of the film *A Kind Of Loving*, complete with an overbearing mother-in-law. In the new scenario, the beleaguered husband Johnny leaves his job in search of a better position but ends up losing his home and his wife. Not for the first time, Davies was reminding us of his reservations about upward social mobility.

LOVE ME TILL THE SUN SHINES

One of Dave's more memorable rock outings of the period, this recalled the early Kinks' R&B, but still fitted in unobtrusively on the album, with lots of infectious clapping and some solid rhythm playing by Quaife and Avory.

LAZY OLD SUN

This was one of more unusual tracks on the album, with Davies speculating on the sun, in the same way that he would later ponder the meaning of 'Big Sky'. His vocal fades in and out of prominence and the drone effect, produced by the mellotron, adds a suitably atmospheric touch. The raga tinges are juxtaposed to a bizarrely overdramatic brass section, which would not have sounded out of place in a spaghetti Western.

AFTERNOON TEA

More light relief from Ray as he adopts a Noel Coward persona on this decidedly English tale of platonic love among the tea cups. The mood is affectionate nostalgia rather than finger-pointing satire.

FUNNY FACE

This harder-edged Dave Davies track was much needed at this juncture in the proceedings. His psychotic humour comes to the fore, as he imagines a love locked away in a mental home surrounded by doctors and frosted glass. The chaotic coda was reminiscent of the Who's more raucous offerings from the same period.

END OF THE SEASON

This was the oldest track on the album dating back to the recordings for *Face To Face* in April 1966. Note the sound effects which were once meant to be an inextricable part of that record. Davies uses the close of a cricket season as a metaphor for the end of a relationship. Interestingly enough, the song recalled the style of the New Vaudeville Band, then about to hit big with the international hit 'Winchester Cathedral'. They might well have enjoyed a hit with this track, but instead it was covered by the Uglys, who narrowly missed the charts, despite receiving some reasonable airplay.

WATERLOO SUNSET

Saving one of his classic songs for an unexpected finale, Ray provided an exercise in how to make a great record. With a descending bass line opening, similar to 'Sunny Afternoon', and some enticing concluding harmonies, assisted by Dave, Rasa and Pete Quaife, the song emerged as one of his best of the decade. Producer Shel Talmy originally employed Nicky Hopkins for some haunting piano work, but Ray was ambivalent about the recording. Eventually, he entered the studio and laid down an alternate take which was supposedly used on the record, although Talmy emphatically denies that this was the case. What is certain is the quality of the piece, a lovely lyric, glamorising the mundane with a genuine sense of wonder. "I read the words to 'Waterloo Sunset'," Davies recently recalled. "It doesn't mean anything. But when you hear the record, it means a lot. All the colours are there. I had to go into the studio and produce that record because that made up for me not being a painter. When I did the mix, I came down to Waterloo Bridge, to see if it worked. It was my substitute for not being able to paint it."

THE KINKS
LIVE
AT KELVIN HALL

LIVE AT KELVIN HALL

RELEASED: JANUARY 1968

ORIGINAL UK ISSUE: PYE NPL 18191 (MONO)/NSPL 18191 (STEREO)

Recorded live at Glasgow's Kelvin Hall on 1 April 1967, this album was originally intended for release during the summer of love but it was postponed in order not to clash with the new studio work *Something Else By The Kinks*. However, the original release date was adhered to in the USA, where the album appeared under the title, *The Live Kinks.* The UK pressing is superior, with the tracks running into each other, rather than being artificially banded. Although the work arguably captures much of the excitement of a Kinks' show of the period, the actual recording is a disappointment. More attention seems to be focused on the audience than the group and most of the performance is drowned by incessant screaming. Record company indolence is evident from the sleeve artwork, which erroneously credits 'All Day And All Of The Night' instead of 'Till The End Of The Day'. At times the package almost resembles rock's first bootleg. A strange slice of audio-verite, complete with fluffed notes and sometime off-key singing, the album remains a fascinating curio, highlighted by the closing medley which combines 'Milk Cow Blues', 'Tired Of Waiting For You' and the 'Batman Theme'.

Full track listing: 'Till The End Of The Day', 'A Well Respected Man', 'You're Looking Fine', 'Sunny Afternoon', 'Dandy', 'I'm On An Island', 'Come On Now', 'You Really Got Me', 'Medley: Milk Cow Blues, Batman Theme, Tired Of Waiting For You'.

THE KINKS ARE THE VILLAGE GREEN PRESERVATION SOCIETY

RELEASED: NOVEMBER 1968

ORIGINAL UK ISSUE: PYE NPL 18233 (MONO)/NSPL 18233 (STEREO)

The crowning achievement of the Kinks' career and their best album by some distance, this was the moment when Ray Davies finally ordered his songs into a work with a single purpose. Arguably, the first real "concept album" of the Sixties (although the term had yet to be coined), this was Davies's version of Dylan Thomas's *Under Milkwood*, a funny and often dark evocation of village life, with a list of colourful and contrasting characters. The work is unified by the elegiacal mood that permeates most of the songs and the sense of longing and regret expressed in the visions of lost childhood, passing time and fading traditions. The album would have made a promising mini-musical – and a far better one than some of the theatrical excursions that would follow in the Seventies. Not for the last time in the Kinks' story, the track selection was subject to change at an advanced stage. The work was originally conceived as a 12-track album, but Ray extended it to 15 cuts at the eleventh hour, deleting 'Mr Songbird' and 'Days', then adding 'Last Of The Steam Powered Trains', 'Big Sky', 'Sitting By The Riverside', 'Animal Farm', 'All Of My Friends Were There' and 'People Take Pictures Of Each Other'. The 12-track version did appear in France, Sweden, Norway, Italy and New Zealand and was even reviewed as such in the *New Musical Express*. We should be thankful that Davies improved the work so markedly, although it would be interesting to sample 'Days' amid the familiar running order. Regrettably, this album sold poorly, despite its evident quality, confirming the notion that the Kinks were still regarded primarily as a singles group by the record-buying public. Now rightly regarded as a classic by Kinks' enthusiasts, the work deserves a better placing in the all-time great album charts beloved of magazines and book publishers.

THE VILLAGE GREEN PRESERVATION SOCIETY

The album opens with a quaint listing of the institutions that should be saved for posterity. Ray casts himself in the role of cultural saviour, although the presence of the American icon Donald Duck alongside such British creations as the *Beano*'s Desperate Dan, suggests that the Anglocentric ideal has already been tainted. "I like these traditional British things to be there," Davies insisted. "It's bad for people to grow up and not know what a china cup is – or a village green. It all sounds terribly serious, but it isn't really. I mean, I wouldn't die for this cause, but I think it's frightfully important."

DO YOU REMEMBER WALTER

Fear of change is followed by nostalgia and regret about the passing of time. Opening with some machine gun drumming, this superb track returned to territory last explored on 'David Watts'. Here Davies's adolescent hero is glorified as an irrepressible Jack the lad, who played cricket in the pouring rain, smoked fags illicitly and was known to every girl in the neighbourhood. The pathos of shattered ideals is fully exposed in the second half of the song, in which Davies imagines his childhood hero fat, married and irredeemably grown up. With a vocal that combines longing and regret, Davies fully captures the potency of adolescent dreams and their obliteration by age, adulthood and mundane responsibility. The result is nothing less than one of his greatest songs of the era.

PICTURE BOOK

This deceptively light-hearted song, complete with quasi-barbershop harmonies and airy acoustic guitar work, was underlined by some darker reflections on the past as the ageing narrator happily skims through a picture book and attempts to recall the best of times.

JOHNNY THUNDER

Here Davies brings a comic book hero to life in his depiction of a character that "feeds on lightning". Unlike Walter, the glamorous Thunder retains his mythological power, although he is never developed as a flesh and blood character and remains sketchily drawn. Another fine tune, complete with some strong harmonies and an enticing arrangement.

LAST OF THE STEAM-POWERED TRAINS

One of the great surprises of the album was this unexpected return to the Kinks' R&B roots. Loosely based around Howlin' Wolf's 'Smokestack Lighting' riff, the track should have sounded out of place on the album, but instead worked extremely well. The steam train analogy fitted well with Davies's view of himself ("I live in a museum") as the curator of Britain's cultural artefacts. Musically, the song was an onomatopoeic exercise, with the harmonica and guitar imitating the rolling of the train, speeding up towards a dramatic conclusion and coda relief. The result was one of the group's better R&B stabs.

BIG SKY

Improbably inspired by a visit to the Midem music festival in Cannes, this song was conceived while Ray watched various music publishers scurrying around while he sat imperiously high above on a hotel balcony. He emerged with a fascinating arrangement and a lyric that exploded the absurdity of human behaviour when set against the vastness of nature. Many listeners have interpreted the Big Sky as symbolic of God. If this is so, then Ray's God is a distinctly impersonal deity, closer to the Victorian notion of the Supreme Being as an inactive force in the universe. "If God's an influence on something, I don't want to tell everyone about it," Davies concluded.

SITTING BY THE RIVERSIDE

Ray Davies has written a number of songs about the pleasure of laziness and this is another attempt to convey the beauty of a quiet life. With a pleasant piano backing, the song reaches a crescendo, complete with intriguing sound effects typical of the post - *Sgt Pepper* period.

ANIMAL FARM

Although the title was borrowed from George Orwell, the anti-urban theme had more in common with H.G. Wells' *History Of Mr Polly*. Nicky Hopkins' delightful harpsichord imbues the track with a stately grace, while Ray's assured and expressive vocal outlines the process of pastoral redemption. One of several candidates for best track on the album, the composition was much loved by Pete Quaife, who would soon be leaving the group for the second and final time.

VILLAGE GREEN

This was the earliest recording on the album, stretching back as far as November 1966. It's intriguing to consider that Davies was tinkering with a project based on this song at such an early date and even more surprising that he suppressed a song of this quality for so long. The harpsichord and woodwind backing are enchanting, while the lyrics satirise the sentiments outlined in the title track. Davies still glorifies village greens and church steeples, but the exuberance of 'The Village Green Preservation Society' has been replaced by a more solemn vocal and a nightmare vision of the community overrun with American invaders. The cheapening of the landscape recalls the satire of 'Holiday In Waikiki'.

STARSTRUCK

Davies's equation of the city with artifice is emphasized here by his female character's failure to distinguish reality from the illusion of stardom. It could have been about a groupie, although the delicate and polite chastising makes this unlikely. Musically, this had a distinct Acapulco-flavouring with some harmonies clearly influenced by the Turtles.

PHENOMENAL CAT

With its alluring flute, woodwind and tambourine backing, this emerged as another of the album's many highlights. An enigmatic fairy tale, the composition had a vaguely Victorian flavour, with shades of Edward Lear and Lewis Carroll. Dave plays the cat at one point, complete with phased vocal effects. The literary aspects were rather spoilt by the misspelling 'Pheonominal' on the album sleeve.

ALL OF MY FRIENDS WERE THERE

Returning to his favourite music hall influences, Davies presents a humorous account of his inability to shake off admirers wherever he goes. There's a neat churchly organ in there which enhances the quizzical nature of the narrator's accidental encounters.

WICKED ANNABELLA

This tale of a wicked witch of the woods featured some of the best guitar playing on the album. The riff recalls the Doors' 'Light My Fire', which is delightfully ironic considering the way the American group blatantly copied 'All Day And All Of The Night' for their second US chart topper, 'Hello I Love You'. Dave Davies relates Ray's black fairy tale with a suitably emphatic vocal and the song concludes on a resounding note with some clever interplay between the drums and guitar feedback.

MONICA

Ray's love of calypso re-emerges on this light but tuneful piece. Ostensibly a love song, it becomes clear quite quickly that Ray is serenading a woman of the night. The whore with the heart of gold theme is subtle enough to go unnoticed, which is precisely what Davies intended. "I like the way I did 'Monica'," he observed. "I think that I explained it enough to me and to various other people. I didn't actually say she was a prostitute, so it can apply to a lot of other people. If you say somebody is a prostitute or hooker, you're restricted."

PEOPLE TAKE PICTURES OF EACH OTHER

The concluding track served as an answer song to 'Picture Book', with Davies satirising the absurdity of taking photographs in order to enshrine the past. "I'd rather have the actual things here not just pictures of things we used to have," he remarked. The inspiration for the song came from a wedding that Ray had recently attended. "It was only a little wedding in the country," he remembered. "We walked back from the church. The guy was in the navy – and he put a flag up in the back garden... and they all stood there and they took a picture. And then she got the camera and took a picture of him, and he got the camera and took a picture of her... that's strange. That's where that came from. I just got the line and then built on that." In adding music to the composition, Davies obviously had the nuptials in mind when he introduced what sounded like a cross between a Greek wedding song and a Cossack dance.

ARTHUR OR THE DECLINE AND FALL OF THE BRITISH EMPIRE

RELEASED: OCTOBER 1969

ORIGINAL UK ISSUE: PYE NPL 18317 (MONO)/NSPL 18317 (STEREO)

Although they had already recorded a thematic work with their previous album, this is generally hailed as the first Kinks' "rock opera". The vogue term was a little unfortunate as it immediately provoked comparisons with the Who's recently released *Tommy*. Compared to the theatrical splendour of Townshend's work, Davies's effort resembled a village fete production. The subject matter was clearly a key problem. Instead of a deaf, dumb and blind kid who turns his handicaps to messianic advantage, Davies offered the prosaic tale of a working man whose life achievement was emigrating to Australia. If the story line was less than arresting on paper and the forced allegory between Arthur and the decline and fall of the British Empire awkward, there was still much to admire. The production was strong and it was evident that considerable care had been taken with the recording. In other respects, though, the album could and should have been much better. By drawing on the true story of his brother-in-law, Davies promised a work of great pathos, but much of the album was bogged down by dull and laboured songs, specifically written to expand the British Empire theme. If only Davies had concentrated on developing the character of Arthur and composing songs dealing specifically with his life and aspirations like 'Shangri-la' rather than throwing in fodder like 'Mr Churchill Says' and 'She Bought A Hat Like Princess Marina', he might have produced one of the greatest albums of the era. Instead, the work sold poorly and was regarded more as an intriguing curio than an undisputed classic. Although still hailed by some as representative of Davies at his writing peak, *Arthur* remains frustratingly anti-climactic. Despite its greater unity of design, it is a far less impressive album than either *The Village Green Preservation Society* or *Something Else*.

VICTORIA

A sprightly opening number to the album, this effectively sets the scene for Davies's nostalgic/satirical observations on English society. He conjures up an idyllic vision of Victorian England, complete with village greens and stately homes. Despite the subject matter, the instrumentation is hard-edged and noticeably modern, with Dave's sinewy lead cutting between the clarion brass. The overall production is noticeably strong too.

YES SIR, NO SIR

The unquestioning obedience of the military minion is the subject of this song, which again combines brass with lead guitar reasonably effectively. Shifts in tempo, pace and narrator make for interesting listening, but all too often Davies appears to be trying too hard to fit the song into the narrative with unconvincing results.

SOME MOTHER'S SON

The harpsichord, always a favourite additional instrument for the Kinks, is employed during the opening to this anti-war anthem. Although the plaintive approach works up to a point, the lyrics underline that Davies is no Rupert Brooke. The sentiments also sound forced, a consistent failure with Davies when he becomes too detached from his subject matter.

DRIVIN'

Here Davies sounds much more confident and impressive, recalling actual incidents from his childhood that still have resonance in his life. His titular anti-hero Arthur was fortunate enough to own a car during the Davies's childhood years and Ray recalls those moments of escape when they left North London for a drive in the country. He relishes the picnic basket, cataloguing its contents in hungry anticipation and seems to take particular satisfaction at leaving various members of his extended family at home. The convincing lyrics are matched by a sumptuous melody and some amusing percussive flourishes from Mick Avory at the end of the song.

BRAINWASHED

This track effectively reiterates the theme of 'Yes Sir, No Sir'. Although adequate as a linking song in the story it adds little to the plot lyrically and is less than average as a track in its own right.

AUSTRALIA

The first half of the album closes with this amusing tour de force, with Ray singing the title with all the subtlety of a costermonger. Although the song probably wouldn't have worked outside the limited context of this album, it works well when viewed as a potential track from a musical. There's a grand mixture of musical styles, including Caribbean influences, a surf section and, most impressive of all, an extended rock/blues guitar section from Dave which provides a striking contemporary edge.

SHANGRI-LA

A stark acoustic guitar frames Ray's deliberately executed vocal as he unveils the centrepiece of the entire album. Over five minutes in length, the song emerges as one of Davies's best from the period. His ambivalence towards his subject is evident throughout as he takes an alternately affectionate and sardonic look at cosy middle class aspiration. The satire is made more brutal by the condescending observations on suburban life and the blandness of the little man who accepts his lot with stoical resignation.

MR CHURCHILL SAYS

Like the other political songs on the album, this was a terribly unconvincing attempt to step forth from familiar lyrical territory to observe war-time attitudes from an ironic angle. Davies even quotes from Churchill's speeches in a hammy voice that is merely irritating. Distanced from the subject matter, he lacks conviction. "Obviously, I wasn't

around when that was happening," Davies admitted, "but I know people who were. And I can remember Churchill being Prime Minister... we had Mr Churchill and good old Churchill told us what to do." Ultimately, this was little more than a piece of ephemera.

SHE BOUGHT A HAT LIKE PRINCESS MARINA

This was even worse, coming across as little more than second rate musical fodder made more embarrassing by Davies's excruciating attempt at an upper class accent. While the notion of the proletariat aping the royals was mildly interesting, the song ultimately sounded like an irksome filler.

YOUNG AND INNOCENT DAYS

The old theme of nostalgia for a lost past brought a more sedate mood to this section of the album but, in truth, Davies has written far better songs than this on the same theme.

NOTHING TO SAY

As a comment on working-class fatalism and the lack of communication between the generations, this was a pretty pessimistic composition. The upbeat production is arresting enough, but the material lacks depth.

ARTHUR

The album ends with this bathetic and pathetic account of the trials and tribulations of Arthur. Recalling the fate of his brother-in-law, Dave Davies was moved to tears following the session. Musically, it was another playful piece, with Ray even attempting some yodelling. A gospel chorus brings proceedings to a suitably over-dramatic close.

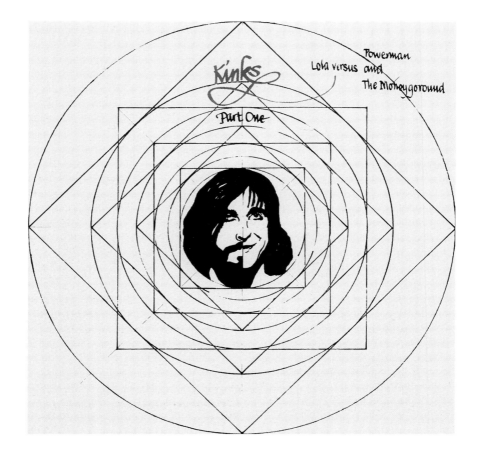

THE KINKS PART ONE – LOLA VERSUS POWERMAN AND THE MONEYGOROUND

RELEASED: NOVEMBER 1970.
ORIGINAL UK ISSUE: PYE NSPL 18359

The first Kinks' album of the Seventies was their coldest and most bitter offering to date, with Ray Davies taking a scalpel to the music industry and cataloguing a decade that had seen him enjoy and suffer pop star fame accompanied by interminable financial and business disputes. Fortunately, his frustrated adventures were marked by several songs of sardonic humour and he emerged here as a much older, wiser and bitter man than previously imagined. The new decade also brought another shift in the group's personnel and sound. Keyboardist John Gosling was recruited, initially on a trial basis, but before long the group would be reinvented as a quintet. With extensive touring at larger venues, they felt the need for a heavier hard rock sound which was evident on several tracks on the new album. While Dave was content to play the rock guitarist, his brother was still haunted by the desire to make concept albums. The clumsy title of this album betrayed Ray's tendency to think in grandiloquent terms, even when the subject matter was mundane and the concept only partly worked out. Significantly, there was no Part Two to this record.

THE CONTENDERS

The album opens with the folkish refrain of 'Got To Be Free' before segueing into the hard rock of 'The Contenders'.

This was clearly the start of a new phase for the Kinks, with a more bombastic sound, far removed from the pastoral subtlety of their previous three albums. Their return to America after years in exile clearly had a profound impact on their approach, encouraging Dave to push for a more muscular sound.

STRANGERS

Written by Dave Davies, this reflective lyric on the human condition was backed by some thumping drum work from Avory and an organ accompaniment by new boy John Gosling.

DENMARK STREET

Ray's paean to the home of Tin Pan Alley was the first of several songs satirising the music business. His dig at music publishers here was accompanied by a singalong melody. While many writers would have expressed the theme as a dirge or angry protest, Davies prefers to stand back and smile sardonically at the absurdities of the pop game.

GET BACK IN LINE

This track was inspired by a moment prior to pop star fame when Davies found himself in a dole queue. The song also attacks the abuse of union power, a reactionary view but understandable in the context of Kinks' history as the American Musicians' Union had been instrumental in banning the group from appearing in the USA for several years.

LOLA

This was the most famous Kinks' song of the period and probably their most instantly recognizable. The riff is as distinctive as 'You Really Got Me' and the theme captured the imagination of an audience, part amused, part fascinated and part mystified by transvestism. Normally, a song this explicit might have risked a ban by the BBC, but the corporation's concern did not extend beyond an insistence that the name 'Coca Cola' be altered on the single version. Here, we can hear the original reference to Coca Cola in all its glory. As with the later and far more explicit Lou Reed hit, 'Walk On The Wild Side', programmers found transvestism far more acceptable than sex, as long it was couched in coded references that would not alarm listeners. In an age when Danny LaRue was a star and comedians regularly dressed as women on stage, 'Lola' was at worst seaside postcard naughtiness, with a sly wink towards perversity in the sexually ambiguous conclusion: "I know what I am and I'm glad I'm a man – and so is Lola". In interviews of the period, Ray remained characteristically coy about the theme: " 'Lola' is a real person and a very good friend of mine, a dancer actually. I'm not going to tell you what sex the person is, though. It's a joke song but it's very real. I think that sex is very unimportant in friendships. That's why I wrote the song."

TOP OF THE POPS

Davies's satire on the pop industry continued with this masterful aside which managed to pillory the BBC, the *New Musical Express* and *Melody Maker* in the space of a single line. Musically, there were subtle references to the Kinks' early sound, with a riff that alternately recalled 'Louie Louie', 'You Really Got Me' and 'Land Of 1,000 Dances'. The song dramatizes the group's rise to number 1 in the charts, with Ray risking an anti-Semitic ending by uttering in a Jewish voice: "This means you can earn some real money".

THE MONEYGOROUND

This was undoubtedly the highlight of the album and one of the most audacious statements that Davies has ever made on record. Over the previous few years, Davies had suffered managerial and publishing disputes which had culminated in a crucially important High Court action against former manager Larry Page and music publisher Eddie Kassner. In the song, Davies dares to name the characters in the scenario, outlining the tripartite management deal between Robert Wace, Grenville Collins and Page, and complaining about the supposed iniquities of the publishing business by which overseas publishers were allowed to cream off 50% of the profits. The fact that the song was played at a manic pace, like some crazed music hall pastiche, made it sound even funnier. Not surprisingly, the characters mentioned in the song were less than amused. As manager Robert Wace noted: "We didn't see the funny side of that at all. The fact was that Grenville and I never earned a dime from his songwriting."

THIS TIME TOMORROW

When moving away from the abject satire of the music business, Davies's songs sounded less convincing on this album. This speculation on the future was adequate fare but far below the quality of the more acerbic compositions herein.

A LONG WAY FROM HOME

This track fitted in vaguely with several of the other songs on the album, as it reflected on the rise of a working-class kid to a position of *nouveau-riche* wealth. The title also betrayed the insecurities felt by the travelling rock band.

RATS

This slab of hard rock from the pen of Dave Davies was a brutal and largely undistinguished attack on conformity. Both the lyrics and vocal are buried by the high decibel instrumentation.

APEMAN

Although obviously a novelty song, this track had more serious undertones, with Davies complaining about pollution and voicing the need to return to a simpler way of life. The calypso backing was reinforced by Ray's decision to sing the song in a Jamaican accent, the execution of which sounded rather like those politely racist Caribbean parodies broadcast by satirists on television during the early Sixties. His forced patois at least enabled him to get a swear word past the censors with the disguised phrase "foggin' up my eyes".

POWERMAN

A cascade of acoustic and electric guitars introduced Davies's concluding song of corporate greed, embodied in Powerman. This was another revealing account of Davies's disillusionment with the music business, summed up in that memorable complaint: "He's got my money".

GOT TO BE FREE

The album closes with a complete version of its opening refrain, a moving plea for personal freedom set beside an attractive folk-flavoured melody. It provided a quiet but impressive conclusion to a work that revealed the Kinks at a new musical cross-roads.

"PERCY"
starring HYWEL BENNETT
with guest stars
ELKE SOMMER & BRITT EKLAND
Soundtrack from the film by
THE KINKS

PERCY

RELEASED: MARCH 1971

ORIGINAL UK ISSUE: PYE NSPL 18365

The final new Kinks' album on Pye was this hotch potch collection of tracks from the soundtrack of *Percy*, a comedy whose central theme was the amours of a man given a penis transplant. Considering the subject matter, one might have expected an album of saucy songs in the vein of 'Lola', but instead Davies offered several reflective and serious compositions, strangely out of place in their context. With many of the tracks accompanied by a full orchestral section, much of this sounded less like a Kinks' recording than a Ray Davies solo outing. Pye wisely issued the best tracks on an EP which was the preferable format for this selection of songs. As an album, it was incoherent and insubstantial, padded out by instrumentals and typically bland movie soundtrack material. Not surprisingly, the group's US record company Reprise elected not to release the album on the grounds that it had no commercial potential and too many instrumentals.

GOD'S CHILDREN

This spellbinding melody was clearly the highlight of the entire album. With the penis transplant at the back of his mind, Davies decided to write a serious song about the limitations of technology. His plea for a return to Edenic innocence was powerful and moving and arguably the closest he has come to writing a religious song. The acoustic accompaniment, beautifully enhanced by Stanley Myers' orchestral arrangement, was also striking. On reflection, it was regrettable that a track of this quality was lost on such an inconsequential work.

LOLA

This new instrumental version of 'Lola' allowed Dave Davies to show off his guitar work to splendid effect. Alas, Gosling's organ accompaniment sounded like it had been sampled from a hammy quiz show. The track ended in bombastic fashion with full orchestral accompaniment.

THE WAY LOVE USED TO BE

Another clue to what Ray Davies might have sounded like as a soloist, this plaintive composition worked pretty well with Myers' orchestral backing.

COMPLETELY

Like a grit in the syrup, this instrumental 12-bar blues was about as dull as you could possibly imagine.

RUNNING ROUND TOWN

An instrument fragment, this was a one-minute interlude.

MOMENTS

With guitar work reminiscent of the Merseybeat era, this was a reasonably good neurotic love song, with Ray's anguished vocal dramatized by the additional orchestration.

ANIMALS IN THE ZOO

With some derivative playing recalling the rhythm of 'Willie And The Hand Jive', this sounded suspiciously like a thematic re-run of 'Apeman'.

JUST FRIENDS

This was an unusual arrangement, opening promisingly with a music box and harpsichord with a strong Elizabethan influence. Unfortunately, the novelty Noel Coward spoof spoiled what might otherwise have proved an intriguing composition.

WHIP LADY

Another one-minute instrumental interlude of dubious merit and best forgotten.

DREAMS

This was one of the better cuts on the album, with a strong commercial melody, decent lyrics and some interesting time signatures. It could have been put to much better use elsewhere.

HELGA
Another instrumental, this time offering some pleasant acoustic guitar, although it fails to work outside the context of the film.

WILLESDEN GREEN
This bizarre country & western pastiche, featuring London place names instead of American ones, was the first and last time that John Dalton would sing lead on a Kinks' record. Mildly amusing as a one off but not recommended for repeated listening.

GOD'S CHILDREN – END
A 25-second instrumental refrain of the excellent opening track concludes the album.

MUSWELL HILLBILLIES

RELEASED: NOVEMBER 1971

ORIGINAL UK ISSUE: RCA VICTOR LSP 4644

The first Kinks' album for RCA was a significant departure for the group with a stripped-down sound far removed from the harder rock evident on their last album. Another surprise was the incorporation of a three-piece brass section, the Mike Cotton Sound, which would continue to be used for Davies's theatrical excursions over the next few years. 1971 was an age of supergroups, sentimental and serious singer-songwriters, progressive rock exponents and heavy metal harridans. Predictably, the Kinks fitted into none of these categories and, rather than taking the easy route by becoming a stodgy hard rock outfit, they were obliged to follow Davies's muse and turned inwards. This was their most parochial album to date, a sort of updated 'Dead End Street' documenting the struggle of ordinary men and women devoid of glamour. The revealing cover shot featured the group drinking at North London's Archway Tavern, a pub where Ray spent much time listening to Anglo-Irish country & western music. That style of music, with its overt Americanisms mutated into a style that bordered on parody to the purist, inspired Ray to try something similar. The result was a strange fusion of turn-of-the-decade UK rock, fused with American country rock influences and an old-styled brass band, Salvation Army sound. Such a pot pourri of styles made for odd listening at times, yet the whole was an intriguing concept. At times it was difficult to empathise with the subject matter, especially when Davies allowed his comic vision to turn cruel and attempted to over egg the vocals with affectations. But there were some strong moments of pathos on the album and the unrelenting build up of urban vignettes was ultimately persuasive and arresting. Here were tales of alcoholism, anorexia, mental illness, disenfranchisement and alienation, often related in a flippant, carefree tone that made you ponder about the relationship of the songwriter to his subject matter. Davies's old stand-by – working class fatalism – underpinned most of these stories in song, creating a mood that was at once warm and disconcerting.

20TH CENTURY MAN

Here, Davies extended his canvas to satirise the entire twentieth century. Like some disgruntled Victorian reincarnated in a forbidding age, Davies damns modern painters and dramatists and seeks refuge in the past. Nearly six minutes in length, the song was notable for some strong bottleneck guitar work and a mid-section that Ray sang in a distinctly folk-cellar voice. The UK division of RCA found nothing on the album that could possibly be released on single, but the Americans issued an edited version of this cut. Not surprisingly, it failed to chart.

ACUTE SCHIZOPHRENIA PARANOIA BLUES

'20th Century Man' had included the lyrics "I'm a paranoid, schizoid product of the twentieth century" and here Davies made an entire song out of that line. It's an amusing tale of comical paranoia ending with a fear of the tax man, an allusion that sounds convincingly autobiographical. According to Ray, the song was

inspired by a friend of his father's and later embellished for humorous effect.

HOLIDAY

With some affected blues intonation, Davies glorifies the working man's escape from the city, a theme last visited on 'God's Children'. Here there is a comic ending, with the narrator suffering sunburn and sewage pollution and requiring a second holiday to compensate for the first.

SKIN AND BONE

This could have been a serious song about anorexia, but instead Davies decided on a comic romp, similar in theme and tone to 'Bony Maronie'. At once novel and sarcastic, Davies pokes fun at fake dieticians and leaves the former 16-stone girl friendless and alone, abandoned by her peers because she is now too thin.

ALCOHOL

With a Salvation Army backing, this story of a respected man's fall into alcoholism was again treated as a subject for amusement with Davies gleefully reeling off a list of drinks that his protagonist enjoyed.

COMPLICATED LIFE

Originally titled 'Suicide', this was an ironic look at a troubled individual forced to take minimal exercise and ordered to relax by his doctor. He eventually atrophies and ends up a social vegetable. Despite the bleak tone, the story is related flatly without inviting sympathy, accompanied by a country & western steel guitar backing and an affected American accent from Ray mid-way through.

HERE COME THE PEOPLE IN GREY

Dave Davies plays a more prominent role in the harmonies here and also offers some striking bottleneck guitar work. The rest is a familiar tale of Davies's aversion to bureaucracy marked by an enduing fear of property repossession.

HAVE A CUPPA TEA

Inspired by the Davies brothers' grandmother, who lived till she was 98, this was an engaging and quaint little song, typical of Ray at his most understated. Who else would write a tribute to the benefits of drinking tea? With snapshots of his childhood family life, Davies credits tea as the ultimate panacea and apparently a cure for hepatitis, tonsillitis and insomnia.

HOLLOWAY JAIL

The local women's prison is featured here as Davies relates the story of a women who takes the rap for her spiv lover and is incarcerated. Dave provides some of the best guitar work on the album on this number.

OKLAHOMA USA

With a concertina backing, Davies relates the story of a downtrodden woman whose only escape from the drudgery of life is the fantasy of being a Hollywood movie star.

UNCLE SON

This tribute to a hard-working man, exploited by the political Left and the Right, was another of the album's more memorable songs. "Uncle Son was an uncle of mine who worked on the railway," Davies recalled. "Most of the people I know in life are just ordinary people like Uncle Son. They're not extremely talented." The fate of his uncle, who subsequently died from tuberculosis, gave the song a personal resonance and there was a note of genuine affection in Ray's valediction: "Bless you, Uncle Son, they won't forget you when the revolution comes".

MUSWELL HILLBILLY

The final track on the album was a country romp, whose theme was similar to that of 'Oklahoma USA'. Like the woman in that song, the "Muswell Hillbilly boy" dreams of a fictional America as seen through the movies. The song also evoked strong memories of Ray's childhood years, including references to the family's move to Muswell Hill and a cameo appearance for the legendary Rosie Rooke. "She used to be my mother's best friend when she was about 16," Davies recalled. "They used to walk up the Holloway Road and all the boys whistled at her because she was very big and well-endowed and nice and shapely. She had a very sad life, and she never felt fulfilled as a person."

EVERYBODY'S IN SHOW-BIZ, EVERYBODY'S A STAR

RELEASED: SEPTEMBER 1972

ORIGINAL UK ISSUE: RCA VICTOR DPS 2035

The first official double album of the Kinks' career was a combined studio and live work. Erratic in quality, it was not without its merits. Ray Davies had originally conceived the entire package as a promotional movie and even filmed several hours of footage of the group, which was later pared down to a 45-minute documentary. Unfortunately, RCA rejected the idea as uneconomical so we were left with an album, minus the visuals that Davies so wanted. Nobody could say that the studio album lacked cohesion – at least in its subject matter which focused almost obsessively on the problems of life on the road, with a special emphasis on travel and diet. Another unifying factor was the isolation of stardom, a theme tackled on the album's finest two songs: 'Sitting In My Hotel' and 'Celluloid Heroes'.

The live section of the work was recorded at Carnegie Hall, New York, on 3 March 1972. Conspicuous for its avoidance of classic Kinks' hits, it nevertheless captured a period when the group was a party on wheels and their shows were dominated by singalongs and self-conscious lapses into vaudevillian whimsy, complete with snatches of show tunes and cabaret evergreens.

HERE COMES YET ANOTHER DAY

This jaunty tune about life on the road was a reasonable opening track revealing an interesting fusion of Kinks' guitar rock and the brass of the Mike Cotton Sound.

MAXIMUM CONSUMPTION

With Dave Davies as second vocalist, this was the first of several songs on the album dealing with food. It was typical of Ray to concentrate on such a mundane theme. At one point in the song, he even employs a sustained metaphor of himself as a high grade car.

UNREAL REALITY

With the Mike Cotton Sound turning on the vaudeville effects, Davies offered a quizzical composition about the failure to distinguish between fantasy and reality. The Kinks get lost somewhere in the arrangement, with Dave Davies's contribution virtually negligible.

HOT POTATOES

Following an opening snatch of guitar vaguely reminiscent of 'My Sweet Lord', Ray returns obsessively to the subject of food – this time providing an extended dissertation on the pros and cons of hot potatoes.

SITTING IN MY HOTEL

This was one of two, maybe three, indispensable tracks on the album. With a stark piano accompaniment, Davies offers a charming melody and thoughtful lyric about the isolation resulting from stardom. Sitting alone in his motel room, the narrator imagines the reactions of old friends to his wealth and fame. It is at once self-deprecating and self-analytical. Perhaps the most surprising aspect of the song is the oblique way in which it comments on the Kinks' tarnished role in the Seventies rock pantheon. Resolutely unfashionable, Davies documents his increasing tendency to write "songs for old vaudeville revues" to the mystification of everyone around him.

MOTORWAY

With a trenchant country inflexion, this was, amazingly enough, the third song on the album with a culinary theme. This time the subject was the state of motorway food. The song was about as arresting as its subject matter.

YOU DON'T KNOW MY NAME

Just as the album was flagging a little, Dave Davies added some passion to the proceedings with yet another song about life on the road. The biggest surprise here was an unexpected flute and piano break in the mid-section where you would normally expect a guitar solo from Dave.

SUPERSONIC ROCKET SHIP

This was extracted as a single and provided the Kinks with a most unexpected Top 20 hit. Sung in a good-time Calypso style, with a fleeting steel drum for good measure, this was Davies's mild attack on rock star hipness. His answer is to fantasise about a rocketship that will serve as a refuge for misfits and suppressed minorities.

LOOK A LITTLE ON THE SUNNY SIDE

This was one of the more intriguing tracks on the album and served as another oblique comment on the current state of the Kinks' career. Davies casually damns critics, poor reviews and the myopia of the underground press, rubbing salt in their wounds by arrogantly employing an intentionally anachronistic vaudeville arrangement. If the Kinks were seen as unfashionable, then Ray was determined to make them look even more so as a playful comment on the present state of serious rock. He even included his own survival guide ("you gotta laugh, don't let your critics get you down") and expressed the absolute need to retain self-belief in the face of media derision ("you gotta convince yourself that you're not wrong"). Impressive in its audacity, this song hinted at the possibility that Ray might well be sabotaging his career as a perverse way of spiting his detractors.

CELLULOID HEROES

The placing of this track after 'Look A Little On The Sunny Side' was surely no coincidence. As if responding to his critics, he magically unveiled a song whose craftsmanship recalled some of the best of his Sixties' work. A precised version was issued as a single and had it stormed the charts, the point would have been rammed home. Instead, it failed on both sides of the Atlantic, as if confirming and reinforcing the worst aspects of Ray's present negativity and cynicism. It was unquestionably one of his most affecting songs of the decade with a strong melody and a thoughtful lyric analysing the complex ambiguities of stardom. In namechecking a litany of Hollywood movie stars, Davies contrasts their mythical status with the flesh and blood figures behind the make-up. Yet the enduring allure of stardom proves so overwhelming that, even after exposing the dichotomy of fame, the narrator cannot resist envying the fantasy life and its Faustian promise of celluloid immortality.

TOP OF THE POPS

The accompanying live album begins deceptively with a familiar minor Kinks' classic in which Dave is at least allowed a decent solo.

BRAINWASHED

Reverting unexpectedly to the *Arthur* album, Davies plucks this less commercial track, which is enhanced by the brass of Mike Cotton and company. As the track closes, an audience member cries: "Ray Davies for president".

MR WONDERFUL

In a camp interlude, Ray sings a 30-second snatch of this musical chestnut, which proves mildly amusing.

ACUTE SCHIZOPHRENIA PARANOIA BLUES

This meaty version of the second track from *Muswell Hillbillies* works well enough in its context and is fairly faithful to the album original.

HOLIDAY

Rather than offering the hits that the audience are baying for, the group throw in another selection from their last album. Played live, you suddenly notice the song's passing resemblance to Dylan's 'Peggy Day'.

MUSWELL HILLBILLY

In introducing the group, Ray mischievously refers to his brother as Dave 'Death Of A Clown' Davies, a nomenclature that serves to remind us of the extent of his brother's fall from grace and weakening influence in the Kinks since the glory days of 1967. Casting himself as Johnny Cash, Ray puts on his country & western accent and the group romp through the finale to their 1971 album.

ALCOHOL

This was one of the most popular live tracks in the Kinks' repertoire. An irresistible crowd pleaser, it allowed Ray to imbibe freely on stage and turn their shows into a party singalong. What was a more serious song on *Muswell Hillbillies* is here transformed into an unambiguous comic drama. Far superior to the studio original, it is complemented by some prohibition period brass and John Gosling's church organ.

BANANA BOAT SONG

This one-minute singalong allowed Ray to involve the audience and show off his West Indian accent. Thankfully brief on record, it was nevertheless a fine comic moment.

SKIN AND BONE

The fifth borrowing from *Muswell Hillbillies* was this bebop boogie which maintained the exuberant pace of the show.

BABY FACE

Dominated by the Mike Cotton Sound, this featured Ray furiously ad-libbing before embarking on an hilarious imitation of Louis Armstrong.

LOLA

While it seemed that the group were about to end the live portion of their album with at least one major hit, this proved yet another tease. It was, in fact, nothing more than a 90-second live coda with the crowd singing the name 'Lola'.

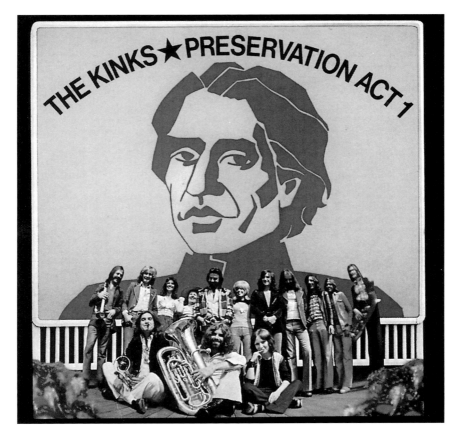

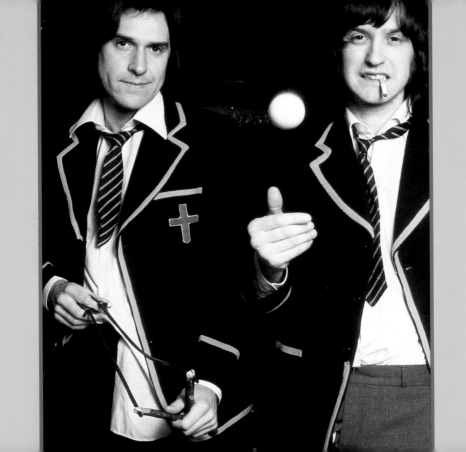

PRESERVATION ACT 1

RELEASED: NOVEMBER 1973

ORIGINAL UK ISSUE: RCA VICTOR SF 8392

After *Muswell Hillbillies*, Davies busied himself with a stage production of *The Village Green Preservation Society*, after which he lurched headlong into his most elaborate theatrical conceit to date. The ominously titled *Preservation Act 1* presaged a full stage musical which was later taken on the road and performed at rock venues. Critics were at first puzzled by Davies's latest scheme and uncertain how to react to what obviously seemed an incomplete work. Then again, *Lola Versus Powerman And The Moneygoround* had been labelled Part One and a sequel was never mentioned, so perhaps the same would apply to this new venture. In time, the Preservation concept would become an albatross for the Kinks, with a further double album to follow. This first effort was a less rigid affair, with Ray introducing three key characters, the Tramp, Johnny Thunder and Flash. Overall, the material was inconsistent, but there were enough memorable moments to keep die-hards happy.

In 1991, Rhino Records issued both *Preservation Act 1* and *Preservation Act 2* as a double play CD titled *Preservation (A Play In Two Acts)*. The effect was a bit like viewing Shakespeare's *Henry IV Pts 1&2* as a single ten-act play. Unfortunately, Ray Davies lacked the bard's ability to create a work that could simultaneously work as a single piece and two separate works. Rhino went further with the controversial inclusion of the single-only 'Preservation', which had been used as an opening and closing theme at the later shows. It was a fine track in itself and better than much of the material on the original album, with Dave playing an engaging solo, presumably inspired by Jimi Hendrix's 'Purple Haze'. This was in striking contrast to the original vinyl version of *Preservation Act 1* back in 1973, which began on a completely different note, as follows:

MORNING SONG

No Dave Davies guitar solos were in sight here. Instead, the musical commenced with a brief choral sequence, augmented by acoustic guitar and brass.

DAYLIGHT

The chorus segues into this first vocal track, which serves as a scene setter. Like a camera, the narrator surveys the scene, observing the various members of the village awakening to prepare for their day. No specific characters are mentioned here, just a steady stream of housewives, clerks, spinsters and babies.

SWEET LADY GENEVIEVE

Sung by the Tramp, one of Ray Davies's favourite personae, this was one of the catchier numbers in the work and was issued as a single. A poignant song of a lost love, it bore a passing resemblance to the Beatles' 'Bungalow Bill'.

THERE'S A CHANGE IN THE WEATHER

Like the famous comedy sketch involving John Cleese, Ronnie Barker and Ronnie Corbett, this offered the contrasting views of the upper-class man, the middle-class man and the working-class man. Unassuming, even in context let alone in isolation, it concluded with a camp vocal from Ray backed by the full chorus.

WHERE ARE THEY NOW?

It seemed that in the world of *Preservation*, the Tramp received all the best songs. This was a quite amusing reflection on images of the past, with Ray taking delight in evoking the Swinging Sixties, namechecking Mary Quant, Christine Keeler Ossie Clark and others, before looking back further to the Fifties and bemoaning the loss of Teddy Boys, coffee bars and CND marchers.

ONE OF THE SURVIVORS

Johnny Thunder, last seen as a characterless superhero in *The Village Green Preservation Society*, is a more rounded figure here. Davies portrays him as an anachronistic survivor from the rock 'n' roll age, grey of sideboards, but still listening to Dion, Jerry Lee Lewis and Johnny And The Hurricanes. The song allows Ray to throw in some Fifties-style vocal inflexions. A different mix and edit on this track appeared on a single.

CRICKET

Another character, the Vicar, is introduced to relate this strained analogy between cricket and religion. Ray's affected voice grates after initial plays of this novelty music hall item. Unashamedly parochial, it is amusing to consider what the American audiences must have made of terms like "googlies", "LBW" and "bowling a maiden over".

MONEY & CORRUPTION/ I AM YOUR MAN

A strong folk influence is evident here as we are introduced to Mr Black, whose capitalist diatribes are intended to awaken the working classes to thoughts of revolution. A false utopianist, Black emerges as the likely villain of the piece, especially given Davies's use of words liked "Fatherland", implying that a dictatorship may well be at hand.

HERE COMES FLASH

This was Dave Davies's long-awaited dramatic cameo, appropriately cast as Flash the bully. Dave is allowed a rare guitar solo here, concluding with a snatch of Khachaturian's 'Sabre Dance'.

SITTING IN THE MIDDAY SUN

The Tramp returns, with an ever so predictable song about escapism and the joys of lazing in the midday sun. Although quite good, the track could hardly compete with earlier songs on similar themes, such as 'Sunny Afternoon' and 'Sitting By The Riverside'.

DEMOLITION

The album concludes with the rise of Flash, the property speculator and evil capitalist. Dave Davies again gets the chance to sing on a track that clearly marks the end of an act, with the plot seemingly only half-developed.

PRESERVATION ACT 2

RELEASED: JULY 1974

ORIGINAL UK ISSUE: RCA VICTOR LPL2 5040

This new double album, over 67 minutes in length, took the *Preservation* concept to its terminable extreme. Easily the longest rock opera to date, it was also one of the toughest to listen to for any length of time. The stagy announcements helped the plot along, but most of the material seemed trapped within its limited format. Between writing Act 1 and Act 2, Davies clearly had a change of heart, resulting in the writing out of the script of Johnny Thunder and a firmer concentration on a single, set idea. Originality was certainly not one of *Preservation's* hallmarks. The simplistic plot line centred on the clash between the dictatorial moral crusader Mr Black and his paste-board adversary Flash. The ending was straight out of Orwell's *1984* – complete with brainwashing, rehabilitation and the final loss of humanity to a totalitarian dystopia, with no hope of change. Musically, there were some pleasant moments but not enough stand out tracks to sustain such a long work. Davies retained the horn players John Beecham, Laurie Brown and Alan Holmes, plus a cast of backing singers. The entire ensemble resembled a touring troupe but despite the fun and camaraderie on the road, there remained a growing feeling that the Kinks were beginning to lose their identity as a group. This was really a Ray Davies musical production functioning uneasily under the ersatz banner of the Kinks. The original issue of this work was released in May 1974 in the US. A two-month delay ensued so that the Kinks would be able to promote the album upon its UK release. It made little difference to the sales figures which were disappointingly poor. Critical reaction was no better, but none of this would be enough to sway Ray from his purpose. The theatrical years had only just begun.

ANNOUNCEMENT

A solitary trumpet heralds a newsflash detailing the rise of the People's Army under the command of Mr Black. The newsreader appears to fluff his line with an impromptu pause, but Davies obviously decided it was good enough to stand.

INTRODUCTION TO SOLUTION

The Tramp takes on a narrative role here, relating scenes of anarchy on the streets. Dave Davies receives a rare opportunity to slip in an aggressive guitar solo towards the end.

WHEN A SOLUTION COMES

Ray switches voices and characters to become Mr Black, seen here plotting his rise in a squalid attic.

MONEY TALKS

Credited to Flash, floozies and spivs, this plodding boogie number saw the roguish property developer and his cronies eulogizing Mammon.

ANNOUNCEMENT

Another newsflash, this time telling us that Mr Black is about to address the nation concerning his new Anti-Corruption Bill. Crowd noises of cheering and clapping can be heard as he is led up to the platform to speak.

SHEPHERDS OF THE NATION

The dictatorial cleric begins his clean-up campaign, denouncing homosexuality, pornography and declining standards. Ray's parodic, psalmodic vocal is accompanied by a suitably rousing rhythm. The song does it job adequately although, in common with much else here, it's difficult to imagine ever listening to any of these numbers in isolation from the rest of the album.

SCUM OF THE EARTH

Although Dave Davies had previously sung Flash's part, Ray now takes over the vocal, a sure sign of his increasing dominance during the theatrical years. Here, he adapts some lines from Shylock's "Hath not a Jew eyes?" speech in *The Merchant Of Venice* as a humorous piece of self-justification in the wake of the new morality.

SECOND HAND CAR SPIV

One of the better tunes on the album, with a decidedly catchy chorus, this was a mini-history of Flash's crony Spiv, a street urchin and dole kid turned car dealer. Now, the dodgy dealer is elevated to the world of finance at the head of Flash's multi-million corporation.

HE'S EVIL

With the expected brass accompaniment, Mr Black offers another party political broadcast speculating on the nature of evil, with Flash no doubt the unnamed subject under discussion.

MIRROR OF LOVE

Ever adept at switching characters, Ray now takes on the role of Belle – Flash's "special floozy". His vocals are expressive and the track is one of the standouts on the album, with clanking keyboards that provide a quasi-fairground feel. The song was issued as a single on two different occasions and one version was an alternate take borrowed from a demo recording.

ANNOUNCEMENT

More news flashes interrupt proceedings. This one provides details of the victory of Mr Black's People's Army over the troops of Flash. The battle takes place on the outskirts of a small village and we are told that no quarter was given by either party, resulting in many casualties.

NOBODY GIVES

Returning to his Tramp persona, Ray waxes philosophical on the frailties of humanity, providing us with a moral history lesson covering the 1926 General Strike and Hitler's military atrocities during the Second World War. The didacticism is a little wearying and the arrangement unspectacular until the dramatic arrival of a stirring string section during the latter part of the song.

OH WHERE OH WHERE IS LOVE?

The Tramp and a cast of do-gooders lament the loss of hope, love and charity in the new age. Ray sings this number with an unnamed backing singer who takes the spot that Dave Davies would usually occupy. Again, this merely indicates the extent to which this is a Ray Davies concept with the Kinks relegated to the level of supporting session musicians.

FLASH'S DREAM (THE FINAL ELBOW)

Opening with the sound of snoring, this somewhat comic/melodramatic piece enters the mind of Flash as he is suffering a nightmare confrontation with his conscience à la Macbeth. Ray adopts a senatorial tone that sounds as though it has been borrowed from Vincent Price. Too stagy for words, this could have been an extract from a school play.

FLASH'S CONFESSION

Awakening from his dream, Flash is force to confront his immoral past and confess his sins. Some interesting sound effects partly salvage a song, which is really nothing more than a clumsy vehicle to push the story along.

NOTHING LASTS FOREVER

In his desperation, Flash turns to Belle for help. Although Ray played this female character earlier, her vocal part here is taken by Maryann Price, another member of the troupe. It's interesting to hear Davies duetting with a female singer under the banner of the Kinks, while the other members can barely be heard playing.

ANNOUNCEMENT

That by now familiar trumpet flare indicates another news flash. The People's Army have now captured Flash, who is to be tried for treason by the People's Court.

ARTIFICIAL MAN

In a languid voice, Ray sings of Flash's defeat and a Mad Scientist's attempt to rehabilitate him for society. Perhaps in a gesture of fraternal magnanimity, Dave is allowed to sing Mr Black's part here. Strong echoes of George Orwell's *1984* are evident , with Flash cast in the role of a Winston Smith, bemoaning his loss of identity and individuality at the birth of a new dystopia.

SCRAPHEAP CITY

The irony of Flash's fall is compounded here as his vulgar property empire is replaced by a concrete jungle characterized by a cold uniformity of design. This lament is sung in country & western style by Maryann Price. Her presence as lead singer, amazingly not even credited on the album, underlines the extent to which Ray was willing to sacrifice the group and himself in pursuing a musical obsession. It was quite amusing to hear a track credited to the Kinks with neither Ray, Dave nor even John Dalton, taking the honours. An alternate take of this song was issued as a rogue single in the US with Ray attempting the Belle role.

ANNOUNCEMENT

The emergence of a totalitarian society is spelt out here when the newscaster announces that a state of emergency has been declared – indefinitely. The population can now look forward to curfews from 9pm to 6am, food rationing, closed shops, petrol, gas and electricity restrictions, the closing down of television stations and places of public entertainment and concomitant loss of civil liberties. All that remains is state controlled radio, which is used to propagandist purpose.

SALVATION ROAD

Following the derivative Orwellian end to the saga, Davies adds a musical coda – the new national anthem. Several musical refrains from the musical are pieced together here and Ray provides an exuberant vocal. So ends the most interminably long and hardest going album in the Kinks' canon.

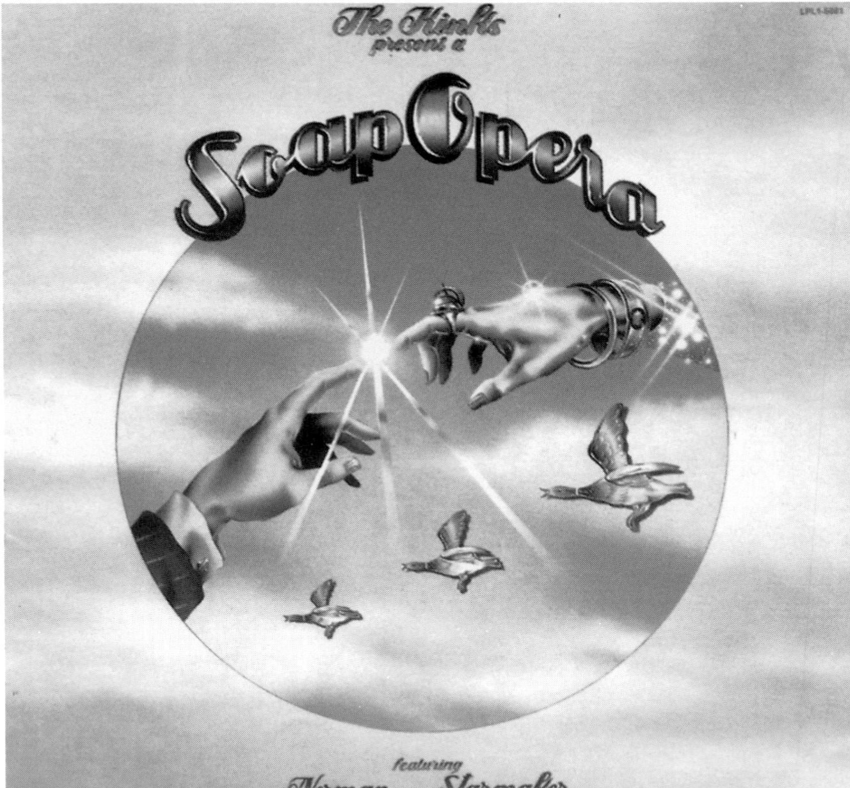
The Kinks
present a
Soap Opera
featuring
Norman
Starmaker

SOAP OPERA

RELEASED: MAY 1975

ORIGINAL UK ISSUE: RCA VICTOR SF 8411

Ray Davies's dogged interest in pursuing theatrical projects turned unexpectedly to his advantage when he was offered the chance to write and appear in a 30-minute television drama, *Starmaker*. The play centred on Norman, a mild-mannered suburbanite who believes that he is a rock star and sets out to make a concept album. As the drama progresses dream and reality become more and more confused and at the close Norman leaves the stage to join the audience watching the Kinks. Although the play was not greeted with plaudits, it provided an interesting insight into Ray's own view of his relationship with the Kinks, whose function as a group had become increasingly marginalized as a result of the *Preservation* concept. Ironically, Davies decided to transform the *Starmaker* idea into a new Kinks album, thereby pushing them further away from their roots as a rock group. The project was an uneasy compromise, weighed down by dull material, much of which testified to Davies's loss of inspiration since beginning the theatrical concept album game. Fortunately, there was a teasingly positive conclusion to the album, as though Davies was deliberately saving the best songs for last to test our patience once again.

EVERYBODY'S A STAR (STARMAKER)

Confusingly, the Kinks began their new album with a title adapted from the name of their 1972 album *Everybody's In Showbiz, Everybody's A Star*. There were elements of the old Kinks' rock/R&B sound here emerging from behind the expected brass backing. This song sets the scene with the Starmaker searching for a suitable subject.

ORDINARY PEOPLE

The Starmaker discovers the embodiment of suburban mediocrity in Norman. As an experiment, he enters his body, exchanging his flashy stage suit for a pin-stripe. Musically, this is less than riveting stuff, but the backing singers throw in some Fifties' style vocals, which distract attention from the song's shortcomings.

RUSH HOUR BLUES

The rock 'n' roll style musical backing is again evident here and there are comic exchanges between the Star/Norman and his wife, played by June Ritchie. This was the first song that Davies had written about commuters since 'Waterloo Sunset', although any other comparisons end there.

NINE TO FIVE

The next scene takes place in Norman's office where the Star discovers the mundanity of 9 to 5 clerical life. Alas, the melody is as dull and ponderous as its subject matter.

WHEN WORK IS OVER

At least, unlike *Preservation*, the songs flow into each other with some slickness. This is another fairly nondescript number detailing the drinking rituals following a day's work.

HAVE ANOTHER DRINK

Like a pub bore, Davies cannot resist extending the drinking theme into another song. On this occasion, though, you can actually hear the other Kinks desperately

attempting to emerge with their own sound in another uneasy musical setting.

UNDERNEATH THE NEON SIGN

The reflection on the impersonal nature of the city is another case of a song which appears adequate in elucidating Davies's theme, but largely bereft of charm or inspiration.

HOLIDAY ROMANCE

The holiday fantasies of the office worker allow Davies to extend his theme and move to a more exotic setting, with the possibility of an extra-marital affair with the shy Lavinia. Ray sings the composition in his Noel Coward voice with a sumptuous backing that works quite well.

YOU MAKE IT ALL WORTHWHILE

This proved one of the more intriguing songs on the album, not least because it confronted the nature of the role-playing as well as focusing attention on the character of Norman's wife. There's a moment of high comedy when the fastidious Star rejects a shepherd's pie only to be rebuked by the wife who insists it is "Norman's favourite". The star resolves to write a tribute to the wife's cooking and when next presented with the prospect of "steam pudding and custard for afters" coos "Darling that would be wonderful", at which point a full chorus intervenes.

DUCKS ON THE WALL

Domestic bliss is interrupted by the Star's neurotic aversion to the ornamental ducks that grace Norman's living room wall. An amusing rock 'n' roll romp follows complete with duck noises. The entire effect is not dissimilar to the work of 10cc. This track was probably the most commercial on offer and was released as a single.

(A) FACE IN THE CROWD

By this point the Star believes that he really is Norman and the gap between fantasy and reality becomes blurred. This is the most plaintive song on the album and probably the best melody on offer too.

YOU CAN'T STOP THE MUSIC

Against the odds, the album closes with four decent tracks in a row. Norman's abdication of stardom and resignation to a life of ordinariness has some of the pathetic resonance of *Arthur*, but Davies prefers to end matters on a more positive note. At the last, it is still argued that everybody is a potential star and in order to ram that point home, the group are allowed to break free with this tribute to the heroes and under-achievers of rock 'n' roll. Like Norman transformed, Dave Davies and company are finally allowed back into the spotlight. Although the brass is still there in abundance, it is now more attractively integrated with the Kinks' sound. For the first time in years, Davies looked to have found a compromise between theatre and rock with a hint that brother Dave might be returning from the sidelines.

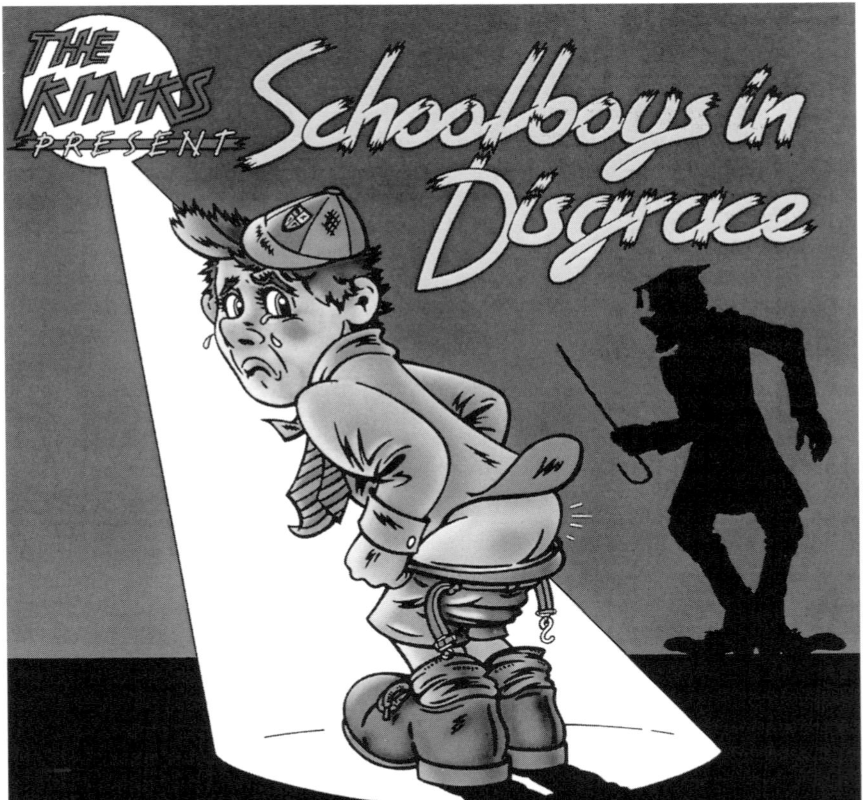
THE KINKS PRESENT
Schoolboys in Disgrace

SCHOOLBOYS IN DISGRACE

RELEASED: JANUARY 1976
ORIGINAL UK ISSUE: RCA VICTOR RS 1028

First issued in America in November 1975, this received its UK release early in the New Year at a traditionally quiet period in the record industry calendar. By now, the association with the Kinks and concept albums was anathema to the British record-buying public. A once hip group now seemed the epitome of uncool and this latest work, painfully accompanied by shots of the Kinks in school uniform, testified to a wilful lack of direction and style. Even by their standards, the subject matter was parochial and mundane, with Ray Davies now taking the story of Mr Flash back to an earlier period covering his schooldays. What looked a disaster on paper actually worked far better than expected. The low-key approach and modesty of ambition made the work more easily appreciated, while the covert autobiographical references and occasional flashes of humour brought a more personal edge to several of the songs. More importantly, this sounded more like a fully-fledged group effort with the musical hall trappings conspicuously absent.

SCHOOLDAYS

This nostalgic longing for a return to the harsh innocence of school life was one of Davies's more affecting compositions of the period. The prominent guitar sound and distinctive presence of Dave on backing vocals grounded the work firmly in the Kinks' oeuvre.

JACK THE IDIOT DUNCE

With an opening piano flourish recalling Jerry Lee Lewis's 'Great Balls Of Fire', this hilarious rock 'n' roll parody was one of the most popular songs during the *Schoolboys In Disgrace* tour. Jack's idiocy is noted at length, but when he accidentally creates a new dance craze, he is no longer vilified but admired. Recalling the genesis of the song, Ray observed: "It was based on a real person in England who failed all his entrance exams but didn't try to commit suicide – he just got kicked out of home. I was amazed when I heard that; I didn't think people did that anymore. He turned up at a relative's house. He said: 'Can I stay here? My father's thrown me out'. Like Victorian times. His father had big ambitions for him and he just didn't make it. The guy was a dummy in school but ended up a rock 'n' roll dancer and a world famous character."

EDUCATION

Davies's history of education embraced the caveman's discovery of speech and writing, man's first foray into travel, the importance of mathematics and finally the limitations of traditional teaching in answering age-old philosophical conundrums. A simply constructed piece, this was broken up by successive organ, guitar and brass solos, culminating in a choral finale. Clearly the centre-piece of the album, it was a fairly good

but far from brilliant song, stretched unnecessarily to over seven minutes in length.

THE FIRST TIME WE FALL IN LOVE

Back to the Fifties with Ray adopting the voice of an American teen crooner for this reflection on young love. While acknowledging the beauty of young romance, Davies typically emphasizes the "difficult emotional pressures and stresses of falling in love". As a pastiche, this worked reasonably well, with echoes of Danny And The Juniors, the Poni-Tails and several others.

I'M IN DISGRACE

The passions and consequences of an adolescent sexual encounter are dealt with in this composition which echoes Dave Davies's own experiences as a teenager. Like the protagonist here, he impregnated a girl and was subsequently expelled for his misdemeanour.

HEADMASTER

The humiliation of the boy is confronted here is he confesses his sex crime to the headmaster, while Dave plays some distinctly Seventies style interweaving guitar work in the background. The song ends with the poignant plea: "Don't make me take my trousers down".

THE HARD WAY

The old Kinks' riff rock sound returns here with Dave letting fly on an impressive guitar solo, while the headmaster promises to lay down the law. Ray's vocal is akin to a pre-punk yowl.

THE LAST ASSEMBLY

With its ominous organ backing and chorus, this opens with a pastiche of the death row song, recalling, amongst others, the mordant 'Green Green Grass Of Home'. The condemned boy finds a solace of sorts singing with his friends at his last assembly. It works well as a country & western pastiche, with a touch of gospel.

NO MORE LOOKING BACK

With a forceful guitar opening from Dave, this was a poignant reflection on the pathetic tendency to revisit old school haunts in the hope of confronting the past. Again, the comparisons with Dave Davies's own history are revealing. After returning from tour, he was known to traipse the streets of Muswell Hill, torturing himself about the girl and child he was forced to leave behind. The composition concludes with the firm conviction that the past cannot be retrieved.

FINALE

The 'Education' anthem returns with everyone joining in the chorus for this curtain-closing one-minute opus.

SLEEPWALKER

RELEASED: FEBRUARY 1977
ORIGINAL UK ISSUE: ARISTA SPARTY 1002

Aswitch of label, a strong promotional budget and a return to their rock roots saw the Kinks re-establish themselves in America with vastly improved sales. This album reached number 21 in *Billboard*, their best showing since the mid-Sixties. Back in Britain, with punk rock about to explode, the group had a tougher road ahead, but there was a general sense of relief among Kinks' aficionados that Ray Davies had, at least for the moment, abandoned grandiloquent concept albums in favour of a straightforward rock album. Beneath the PR hype, however, there were good reasons to be less optimistic. Clearly, he had worked hard on this album, recording around 20 songs, then editing down the selection to nine. Given the number of compositions available, it was disappointing to hear the generally average to poor quality of the best of this material. There was nothing here that came anywhere close to equalling his finest work, though perhaps that was too much to ask one decade on. The Kinks were back, but this was not the group that we had all loved during the Sixties but a strangely soulless unit whose sound seemed as anonymous and antiseptic as many of the mainstream AOR bands dominating the American radio airwaves. Ray Davies's production here was partly to blame. Various members of the group recall how he flogged every song to death with endless retakes until every iota of passion was lost. The homogenized sound that emerged, worsened by the anonymity of many of the compositions, confirmed that all was far from well. It came as no great shock when John Dalton and John Gosling left soon after. At least the Kinks ended the year on a humorous note with the release of a novelty single 'Father Christmas', backed by the decidedly unfestive 'Prince Of The Punks', a forthright attack on singer Tom Robinson.

LIFE ON THE ROAD

With its attractive acoustic opening, this song promised much. The standard rock 'n' roll riff was accompanied by some mildly amusing lyrics namedropping key parts of London from Abbey Road to Praed Street and Pimlico. A suitably safe and solid opening track, this nevertheless sounded a little calculated. The pot pourri of previous Davies' themes – the country runaway adrift in London; the teasing gay reference; the parochial fascination with London place names – seemed merely decorative prods to an old audience that might be tuning in. Davies seemed pretty positive about the merits of the song, which he admitted was written 18 months before. "It was not written specifically for me," he stressed. "It is not autobiographical. Although there are bits of me in it, I wrote it for another character. It's a song I would have liked to have done a whole album about."

MR BIG MAN

This was the only song on the album to feature bassist Andy Pyle, who would shortly replace John Dalton in the line-up. An oblique comment on the isolation and arrogance of stardom, the track was pieced together in the studio and the overall effect is rather leaden.

SLEEPWALKER

Another song inspired by Ray's perennial insomnia, this proved one of the better tracks on the album with improved guitar work from Dave and a sound closer in spirit to the Kinks' better work of the period. Recalling the lyrics, Ray explained: "It's about a vampire, but not the blood-sucking kind. It's more somebody who feeds off of people's lives rather than people's blood – somebody who feeds off their stories. It's like a writer going around getting people to talk in their sleep and then coming out with all of the things they say in their subconscious."

BROTHER

Isolation is again the dominant theme here, punctuated by disillusionment and the sense of a "world gone crazy and nobody gives a damn". Despite the title, the song does not appear to be directed at Dave, but seems more of a general comment on a lack of brotherhood. The string ending was suggested by Clive Davis in the vain hope that a commercial single might be forthcoming.

JUKE BOX MUSIC

This was the strong catchy single that the album clearly needed. The group sound more unified and expressive here, with Dave excelling on backing vocals and playing a fine guitar solo. Ray's arrangement is also less sterile than in other places on the work and the lyric about a woman's musical fantasies recalls the escapism of *Starmaker*.

SLEEPLESS NIGHT

Insomnia once more inspires a song, this time about a man driven insane by desire for his neighbour. Although originally sung by Ray, it was passed over to Dave after he performed a more impressive rendition. Amazingly, this was Dave Davies's first significant lead vocal on a Kinks album since *Lola Versus Powerman And The Moneygoround* way back in 1970.

STORMY SKY

Although competently sung and professionally played, this was another lifeless AOR track lacking the quirky originality of the Kinks at their best. An energetic guitar solo from Dave at the end proves insufficient to rescue the song.

FULL MOON

The overbearingly oppressive feel of the album is emphasized by this nondescript comment on alienation. Ray vainly attempts to muster some passion in his vocal, but it ultimately proves unconvincing.

LIFE GOES ON

At least the album ends on a better note with this cynical but stoical comment on life. The opening lyrics mention a person whose wife has left him, a situation that Davies had recently experienced and no doubt partly explained the downbeat nature of some of this material. Thankfully, there is some evidence here that Ray's old morbid sense of humour has not been completely lost in this arid phase of his songwriting career. At the last, he imagines a darkly comical scenario in which his protagonist attempts to gas himself only to fail due to the utility's cutting off the supply following non-payment.

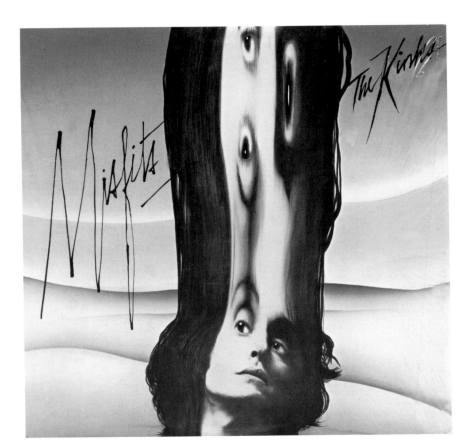

MISFITS

RELEASED: MAY 1978

ORIGINAL UK ISSUE: ARISTA AL 4167

After the AOR coldness of *Sleepwalker*, *Misfits* was a far more human response with some surprisingly strong songs from Davies. The schism between the group's rock leanings and Davies's songwriting was successfully bridged here and although the work was not radical or even consistently excellent, it at least boasted a unified concept with an above average quotient of decent tunes. It was probably the best Kinks' album since before the theatrical forays of *Preservation*. At a time when the group were attempting to re-establish themselves in the US market, the album maintained their high profile. In another sense the work captured the group at a low ebb in morale, with Gosling and Pyle providing their final contributions and the long-serving Mick Avory reduced to playing on only a few tracks.

MISFITS

With its moving Spanish guitar opening and impressive lead vocal, this was one of Ray's best songs for some time. Reflective in mood, it resembled nothing less than an acoustic reiteration of the theme of 'I'm Not Like Everybody Else'. Although Davies had not intended to write a concept album, the "misfit" motif proved applicable to most of the songs herein. "The idea was to make it a lot of tracks that didn't fit with a concept," Davies noted. "But as it wore on and I actually got down to writing lyrics to 'Misfits', things changed. The lyrics and the music to the first verse came out at exactly the same time, and it wasn't until I got into writing the lyrics for the rest of the song that I realized that it was the key track that could tie the whole thing up: it could say a lot about the band, a lot about me, and a lot about the album... So really, though it wasn't intended to be a concept thing, it ended up one simply because it was tied together by one track. If we'd taken that one track off, the rest of the album wouldn't have fitted together."

HAY FEVER

Davies's capacity to write songs about the wilfully mundane reached new depths here. A novelty item on the problems of hay fever sufferers, it was workmanlike and ephemerally amusing. Amazingly, this most superficial of songs required torturous reworking. " 'Hay Fever' we did over and over again," John Gosling told me. "We did it with John Dalton on bass, and then with Andy Pyle on bass. We did it in E, we did it in C, we did it with backing vocals, without backing vocals... it was incredible."

LIVE LIFE

In an era when youth politics was back in vogue in the UK, Davies's characteristic response was to step back and observe. Resolutely apolitical, his panacea was a rather simplistic assertion about the need not to be overwhelmed by bad news. At least Dave Davies is let loose with a meandering guitar solo amid the neurotic observations. Session drummer Clem Cattini deputizes for Avory on this track.

A ROCK 'N' ROLL FANTASY

Arguably the highlight of the album, this was akin to a companion piece to 'Juke Box Music', with both songs focusing on an individual's obsessional interest in music. Here, Davies imagines Dan the Fan, the archetypal Kinks' fanatic who has experienced the group's high and low moments. Originally written as a response to the death of Elvis Presley, the song embraced a new subtext when Ray became fascinated with the behaviour of a guy adjacent to his Manhattan apartment who would spent an entire evening listening to records. "It's a method acting job," Davies said of the completed composition. The song's strong melody encouraged radio play and brought the group their first US Top 30 hit since 'Lola'. As a bonus to collectors, the UK B-side featured the otherwise unreleased 'Artificial Light'.

IN A FOREIGN LAND

Ray's legendary frugality made this tale of tax exile even funnier than intended. Both the arrangement and performance are impressive. This was the oldest composition on the album having been recorded as early as the summer of 1976.

PERMANENT WAVES

Another novelty song based around psychosomatic illness, this begins with some unlikely advice from a doctor who counsels his patient on the benefits of an image change. At a time when the phrase "new wave" signalled the imminent extinction of many so-called rock dinosaurs, Davies merely played on the word "wave" and offered a new hair-do as a riposte.

BLACK MESSIAH

The concept of a black man's God was the mildly controversial subject matter of this song. Reversing the plight of the black American in a white dominated society, Davies presents a comic vision of a "honky living on an all black street"

who is constantly harassed. The trite pleas for equality from all sides ("Everybody gotta work it out") were made more ludicrous by Davies's tongue-in-cheek West Indian intonation.

OUT OF THE WARDROBE

The 'Lola' theme revisited, this tale of husband and wife transvestism was an eye-catching track that was ultimately more interesting for its subject matter than for any musical greatness. At least it allowed Davies to digress on the nature of sexual identity. "People's roles get confused at an early age," he insisted. "They have this sexual thing thrust on them. You're immediately pigeon-holed. You might be a normal person pushed to extremes because you've been crushed by rules, by whatever other people call you. And you might be having a rebellion against what you really are. You see the guy in 'Out Of The Wardrobe' – it might be a phase, a rejection of something that happened at the office. He might not be that way permanently."

TRUST YOUR HEART

Dave Davies received a rare songwriting and lead vocal credit on this rousing number. While Ray pondered political and personal dilemmas in his songs, his anarchic-minded brother was characteristically more single-minded, offering boisterously naive pleas such as "What on earth do we need government for?" The drummer on this track was Nick Trevisick, who also played on 'Rock 'n' Roll Fantasy' and 'Get Up'.

GET UP

Davies's tribute song to the common man was most memorable for his admonition, "Get up off your arses men". The arrangement was noticeably impressive, with Trevisick adding some excellent touches supported by an array of instruments, including acoustic guitar, piano, organ and synth.

LOW BUDGET

RELEASED: SEPTEMBER 1979

ORIGINAL UK ISSUE: ARISTA SPART 1099

Responding with vigour to the new wave fashions dominating the youth market in both the US and the UK, the Kinks rapidly completed their most spontaneous and refreshing album in many years. Davies's decision to record the majority of the work in New York meant that there was a financial incentive to complete the work on time without the temptations to tinker offered by his own studio in London. Away from Konk and invigorated by the pace of life in New York, Davies was able to capture the group's rough edges in a series of snapshot songs about urban life, many laced with his customary droll wit. Back in England, the Kinks were still regarded as passé and the album proved a middling seller. Fortunately, the US market proved more receptive and thanks to consistent touring the group infiltrated the *Billboard* Top 20, peaking at number 11, their best ever showing for a non-compilation album. They were still plagued by line-up changes, this time losing keyboardist Gordon Edwards, who would soon be replaced by the more stable, long-termer Ian Gibbons. With bassist Jim Rodford also establishing himself in the line-up, the Kinks were ready to start the new decade on a positive note.

ATTITUDE

The influence of punk and new wave are immediately evident on this opening track which is played at a blistering pace while Ray adopts a heavily accented London drawl that would not have been out of place on an Oi album. While the lyrics consist of little more than simple slogans, there is no doubting the high energy redolent of the group at a much earlier stage in their career.

CATCH ME NOW I'M FALLING

With a riff caught somewhere between 'Jumping Jack Flash' and 'Satisfaction', the Kinks forge a perfect song for their forthcoming stadium outings. Dave is allowed some extended solos bringing the total running time to nearly six minutes. Significantly for a group now more famous in the USA than in their homeland, the lyrical themes no longer praise village greens or London place names. Instead, Ray namedrops Marvel Comics' hero Captain America.

PRESSURE

Ray's proletarian voice is again evident on this punkish complaint about private neuroses. As Davies noted: "I thought if people get a bit of pressure and talk to somebody about it then somebody else would go off and worry about it. I thought it would be a nice idea for a play – somebody has a bit of pressure and it gets passed on and eventually gets to the president. It's like a disease. The first verse could be about V.D. I wrote it about pressure but it could be about anything else."

NATIONAL HEALTH

Another song about nervous tension and psychosomatic illness, this lists a number of suitable narcotic panaceas before concluding that exercise might be the key to good health.

(WISH I COULD FLY LIKE) SUPERMAN

Released prior to album, this reached number 41 in US charts and was also the first 12-inch single issued by the group. Obviously inspired by the contemporaneous movie *Superman*, it combined two of Davies's favourite themes – fantasy and mundanity. The superhero dreams of the nine-stone protagonist are wittily related, while the music is suitably upbeat.

LOW BUDGET

Partly a vague comment on the state of the economy, this humorous portrayal of a ludicrously penny-pinching individual was one of the most revealing songs on the album. Ray appears to take an ironic look at his own frugality and emerges with one of the best lines of his career: "Don't think I'm tight if I don't buy a round".

IN A SPACE

This mid-paced number, sung in a harsh blues voice, was fairly pedestrian, despite the grand references to space and infinity.

Continuing the urban theme, Davies speculates on over-population, albeit to no great effect.

LITTLE BIT OF EMOTION

The fear of emotion is experienced by everyone in Davies's fictional orbit, including a hard-faced stripper. With a proficient sax solo and pleasant melody, this was reasonable enough, although Ray's child-like voice is a little grating.

A GALLON OF GAS

This comical blues lament on the gasoline shortage then threatening America was wry in places and fitted the general theme of living in the city. When Arista issued this as a single, they chose a longer version of this track.

MISERY

After the various neurotic tales presented herein, Davies devotes an entire song to misery, adding a punchline advising everyone of the need to laugh at themselves. This was another gritty hard rocker, with piano and guitar prominent in the mix.

MOVING PICTURES

Davies's existential vision of life as a movie echoed the theme of 'Celluloid Heroes' from a less sentimental perspective. In keeping with the times, there was a distinctive disco style beat, confirming the Kinks' desire to hit the dancefloors as well as the large arenas.

ONE FOR THE ROAD

RELEASED: AUGUST 1980
ORIGINAL UK ISSUE: ARISTA DARTY 6

The Kinks' second live LP (excluding the segment from *Everybody's In Showbiz, Everybody's A Star)* was a double album culled from no less than 25 shows, spanning the best part of a year. Prior to its release, Arista issued an EP featuring four of the finest tracks: 'David Watts', 'Where Have All The Good Times Gone?', 'Attitude' and 'Victoria'. As well as six cuts from *Low Budget*, Davies carefully included material from the Kinks' golden era, including 'Stop Your Sobbing' and 'David Watts', songs recently made famous by the Pretenders and the Jam, respectively. There was also a chance to sample 'Prince Of The Punks', a track previously available on single only. What was most noticeable about the work was its tightness. Released at a time when the group was peaking as a live act in America, it proved a surprise success, climbing to number 14 in the US charts. The album was also issued on video-cassette.

Full track listing: Opening; The Hard Way; Catch Me Now I'm Falling; Where Have All The Good Times Gone?; Introduction To Lola; Lola: Pressure: All Day And All Of The Night; 20th Century Man; Misfits; Prince Of The Punks; Stop Your Sobbing; Low Budget; Attitude; (Wish I Could Fly Like) Superman; National Health; Till The End Of The Day; Celluloid Heroes; You Really Got Me; Victoria; David Watts.

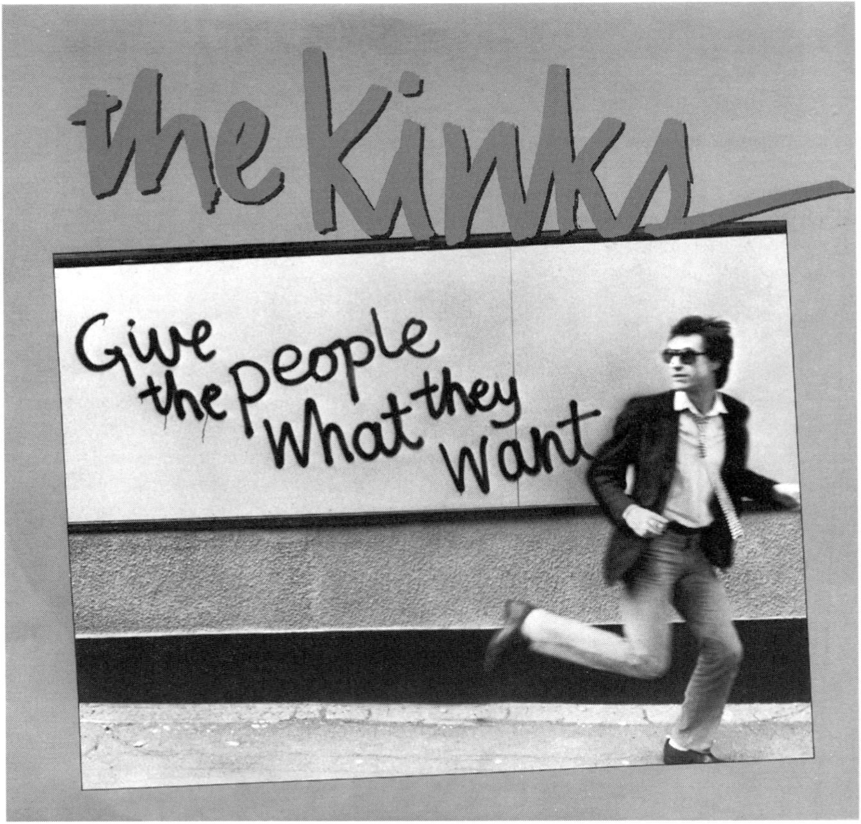
the kinks
Give the people What they want

GIVE THE PEOPLE WHAT THEY WANT

RELEASED: JANUARY 1982

ORIGINAL UK ISSUE: ARISTA SPART 1171

Originally issued in America during August 1981, this album's UK release was delayed for the best part of five months. Predictably, it flopped in Britain, having peaked at an impressive number 15 in *Billboard*. Musically, the work recalled the hard rock of *Low Budget,* confirming the Kinks' evolution into an American stadium band. The album's title was more accurate than ironic, a view reinforced by the profusion of radio-friendly heavy rock guitar solos scattered throughout the disc. Nevertheless, the general quality of the material was good and the work showed none of the weariness that affected the Kinks at times during the mid-Seventies. As ever, Ray Davies's lyrical flights of fancy were notable. Several of the songs herein were thematically intriguing and suggested that beneath an occasionally stodgy hard rock veneer, the songwriter's humour and imagination remained firmly intact. Whatever their critical reputation in their homeland, the Kinks had found a new audience who responded well to their latest material, which was a cut above the work of many of their harder contemporaries.

AROUND THE DIAL

This tale of an heroic disc jockey was obviously aimed at American radio. It serves reasonably well as an aggressive opening track with Dave playing some booming lead guitar while the group playfully indulge in some Beach Boys' style harmonies.

GIVE THE PEOPLE WHAT THEY WANT

A cynical commentary on the audience's equation of violence with entertainment, this was another riff-based song which fitted in well with the group's live set of the period. Davies was inspired to write the song after experiencing the commercial horrors of US television while living in New York.

KILLER'S EYES

The Kinks were travelling by coach from Edinburgh to Glasgow when Ray learned the news that Pope John Paul had been shot. This song was his response. What emerged was a reflective ballad in which Davies sought to enter the mind of the assassin. "There were some quotes from his mother," he recalled. "She always knew that he was going to do something bad one day. I took that attitude in the choruses." A secondary influence was the intense publicity surrounding the trial of the Yorkshire Ripper, Peter Sutcliffe. "I saw his parents being interviewed on television," Ray remembered. "Imagine what Sonia Sutcliffe, his wife, must have gone through not knowing he was a murderer. There's this madness, this attention people want in the Sunday papers. 'Sonia's Terrible Torment'. But they didn't give a shit about Sonia Sutcliffe, she's just good copy."

PREDICTABLE

By contrast, this was one of the lighter tracks on the album – a catchy riff, with wry lyrics sung with a slight West Indian intonation. The attendant promotional video, produced by Julien Temple, was one of the finest of the period and brilliantly brought the song to life with clips of Ray suffering a series of comic disasters.

ADD IT UP

With some reasonable backing vocals and a surprise snatch of synthesizer, this featured Ray playing up his cockney voice on a moderate, if uneventful, track.

DESTROYER

Trading on their illustrious past, the group offered this veritable cornucopia of self references, including the riff from 'All Day And All Of The Night' and the unexpected return of Lola in the lyrics. Emphasizing the stadium gestures, Davies encouraged a boisterous chorus, marked by his booming admonition, "And it goes like this".

The theme of the song also recalled 'Acute Schizophrenia Paranoia Blues' in its concentration on the narrator's neurotic tendencies. Although Ray was reprising old ideas quite blatantly, he felt vindicated when David Bowie chose the same moment to revive the enigmatic figure of Major Tom in the chart-topping 'Ashes To Ashes'.

YO-YO

The subject matter of this song recalled the brilliant 'Shangri-La', with Davies dramatizing the plight of a suburban marriage gone sour. After detailing the wife's boredom and neglect during the first half of the song, he presents a more sympathetic portrayal of the husband who suffers the same fate when his spouse finds a job and he is rendered unemployed.

BACK TO FRONT

This was another standard hard rock item with Ray using the misfit theme in a similar way to 'Predictable', albeit with less imagination and deliberately loutish vocals.

ART LOVER

Sung in a childlike voice, this was one of the more intriguing compositions on the album. Ostensibly a song about the sadness of a man separated from his children, it included strong connotations of paedophiliac intent. The inspiration for the composition came from Ray's own observations of lonely men in Regent's Park, with a touch of Lolita thrown in for dramatic effect. "I have two girls who I don't see," Ray noted at the time. "I'm not allowed to contact them but I can write to them. So I have a lot of feeling for people in that situation."

A LITTLE BIT OF ABUSE

The violence motif running through the album continued with this mildly controversial song about domestic violence. "I used to live down the road from this woman, in Muswell Hill, where I grew up," Ray recalled, "and her face always used to be cut up. But I was too young to realize what it was. Her husband used to come home pissed every night and they were always shouting and fighting. But she stayed with him... until one day she couldn't take it anymore. It's so common."

BETTER THINGS

The album closed on an optimistic note with this upbeat number, which provided the group with a minor UK Top 50 hit, their first chart entry since 'Supersonic Rocket Ship' back in 1972. In many ways, 'Better Things' was a mirror image of 'Days' – Davies's great tribute to a golden era past. Here, he prefers to look forward with a positivity that is both pleasing and unexpected.

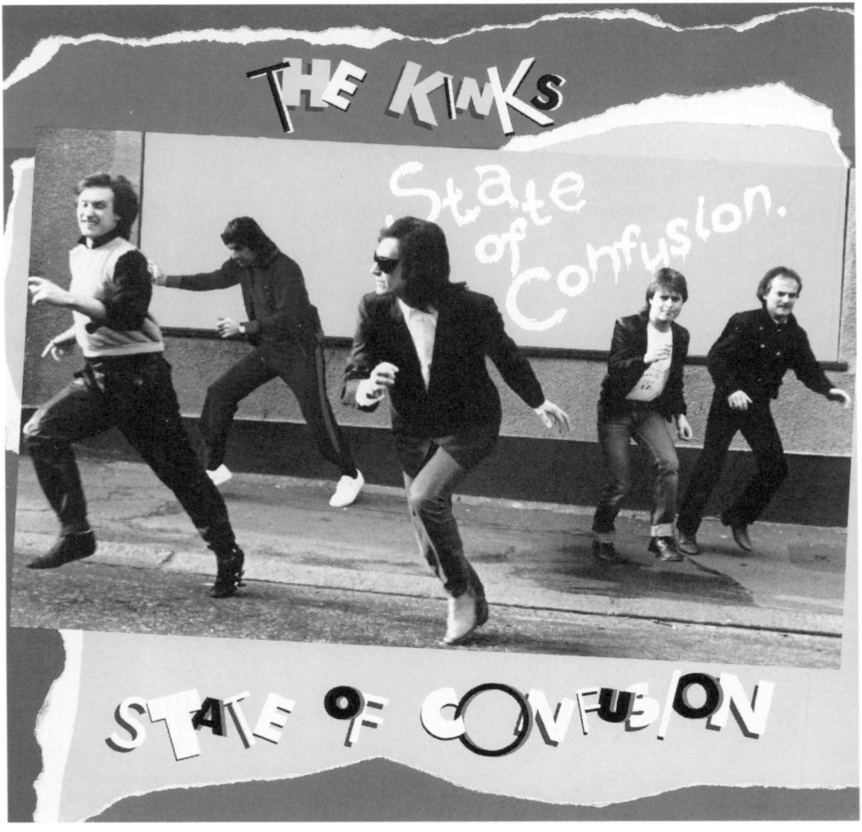
THE KINKS
State of Confusion.
STATE OF CONFUSION

STATE OF CONFUSION

RELEASED: JUNE 1983
ORIGINAL UK ISSUE: ARISTA 205 275

Despite scepticism that the Kinks were turning into a mainstream US stadium band, their work continued to display a thoughtful balance between hard rock crowd pleasers and affective reflections on the human condition. Thanks to consistent touring, they sounded tighter than ever and there was no doubting the quality of their material which had shown a marked improvement since *Low Budget*. This album was the usual pot pourri of Kinks' styles, salvaged by Davies's songwriting. His strike rate was higher here mainly thanks to the inclusion of two excellent singles, the sublime 'Come Dancing' and moving 'Don't Forget To Dance'. The Kinks' high profile Stateside was reflected in continued strong sales with the album peaking at number 12. Unusually, the cassette version of the album featured two extra otherwise unreleased tracks, 'Noise' and 'Long Distance' – a bonus for hard-core collectors. With their twentieth anniversary approaching, the group seemed poised to exploit their recent good fortune and reach a new plateau of critical and commercial success.

STATE OF CONFUSION

As expected, the Kinks began their latest work with a fist-thrusting anthem celebrating Ray Davies's' familiar misfit persona. Like 'Back To Front' and 'Predictable', this was another catalogue of amusing mishaps and domestic chaos.

DEFINITE MAYBE

Bureaucracy gone mad is the theme of this average number, which included some playful backing vocals and a bass riff reminiscent of the Temptations' 'Get Ready'.

LABOUR OF LOVE

Dave Davies opens this track with a Hendrix-like lead guitar break of 'Here

Comes The Bride' before Ray treats us to a sour commentary on modern marriage. His tale of Mr and Mrs Horrible recalls a domestic scenario last seen on 'Yo-Yo', but with a tune that is less than memorable.

COME DANCING

The undisputed highlight of the entire album, this provided formidable proof of Davies's continued excellence as a songwriter. Backed by a snazzy promotional video, in which Ray adopted the persona of his wayward Uncle Frank, the single climbed to number 6 in the US, the group's best performance since 'Set Me Free' back in 1965. Initially, 'Come Dancing' flopped in Britain, but after the promotional video was shown on *Top Of The Pops* during a round-up of US hits, it was re-promoted and reached the Top 20. The charm of the piece lay in Davies's poignant evocation of a lost era when his sisters sought romance at the local palais. The destruction of the ballroom comes to symbolize the death of those romantic dreams but Davies prefers to focus on the innocence of

times past before ending the song with a plea to his sister to re-live former glories. Musically, the composition was also striking, with keyboardist Ian Gibbons providing the fairground organ sound to spectacular effect. Ray's solid acoustic playing, a short electric solo from Dave and an oompah brass coda completed the arrangement.

PROPERTY

The break-up of Ray Davies's second marriage was the obvious inspiration for this song, which proved another highlight of the album. A slight but attractive melody with a hint of synthesizer in the background, this showed off Davies's more sensitive songwriting. It remains a painful observation on the extent to which love can fester into a dispute over property.

DON'T FORGET TO DANCE

The follow-up single to 'Come Dancing', this bittersweet observation of middle-age was another of Davies's stronger melodies. Although a Top 30 hit in the US, it failed to chart in Britain, thereby dashing hopes that the group were about to re-establish themselves as a major commercial force in their homeland. While the song was probably directed at Ray's sister Gwen, the allusion to walking down the street and receiving wolf whistles also recalled his observations on Rosie Rooke, the heroine of *Muswell Hillbillies*.

YOUNG CONSERVATIVES

The death of radicalism on campuses throughout America and the emergence of a more monetary-minded youth prompted this satiric stab at conformity in the Eighties. Although the lyrics namechecked 'A Well Respected Man' and the "fa fa fa" melody echoed 'David Watts', this was a pretty formulaic piece judged by the Kinks' better standards.

HEART OF GOLD

Surprisingly, Davies's favourite track on the album was this light acoustic ballad, partly inspired by Princess Anne's much quoted "naff off" rebuke to intrusive photographers. The recent birth of Davies's daughter Natalie to Pretenders' vocalist Chrissie Hynde was also uppermost in his mind when completing the composition. "I wrote about it imagining I was a photographer," he mused, "but really it was about Chrissie having her first baby. Both she and Princess Anne seem to be quite anonymous people at times."

CLICHES OF THE WORLD (B MOVIE)

More passing social commentary could be heard on this hard rock laden affair in which Davies considers the power of fantasy, a theme already overplayed on songs such as 'Celluloid Heroes' and the entire *Starmaker* episode.

BERNADETTE

Rather than closing the album on a portentous note, Ray allows Dave to resurrect the ghost of 'Lucille' and let rip with one of his Little Richard impersonations. Within the context of the album, this rock 'n' roll excursion works reasonably well and the concluding sax solo provides a fitting coda.

WORD OF MOUTH

RELEASED: NOVEMBER 1984

ORIGINAL UK ISSUE: ARISTA 206 685

Having revitalized their career with 'Come Dancing' and its attendant hit album *State Of Confusion*, the Kinks promptly entered another self-destructive phase while recording this album. After 20 years as their drummer, the much-abused Mick Avory finally ended his stay with the group and was replaced by Bob Henrit. The group's morale was pretty low, with Dave Davies voicing disillusionment over his brother's dominance of the group. After feeling stitched up over the credits on the last Kinks' album, Dave withdrew, leaving Ray to work on another outside project, *Return To Waterloo*. At a time when the group should have been touring incessantly, they instead wasted their recent good fortune and suffered the consequences when this album charted at a lowly number 57 in *Billboard*. The work was arguably no better and little worse than their recent albums, although the number of strong songs may have lessened. Significantly, Dave Davies was allowed to included a couple of his own compositions as the group uneasily sought some kind of compromise.

DO IT AGAIN

The album opened with one of the best Kinks' songs for years. With its emphasis on the need to prove oneself all over again, this was akin to a theme song for the group. Anyone that doubted Davies's ability to fashion classic melodic pop songs needed to look no further than this magic track which uncannily evoked the spirit of a mid-Sixties Kinks single. It deserved to be a major Top 10 hit but regrettably missed out on both sides of the Atlantic. If the Kinks were unable to click with material as strong as this, it was difficult to imagine how they could ever crack the charts again.

WORD OF MOUTH

This bitter comment on the destructive power of rumour was grounded to a basic riff, strongly reminiscent of the Rolling Stones' 'Start Me Up'. Written at a time when Davies's doomed relationship with Chrissie Hynde was a subject of hot gossip in the tabloids, it served as a suitably acerbic riposte. "I wrote 'Word Of Mouth when I got really angry about something," he revealed. "And it hurt. I thought I've got nothing to lose... The rumour and gossip I've been exposed to in the past year – it's the most evil force imaginable."

GOOD DAY

Written during the early sessions for the album, this track was a catalyst in convincing Mick Avory that he was no longer wanted. With old conflicts re-opening, he was replaced here by a drum machine. The song itself was languid in tone and featured several negative images, with Ray conjuring a nuclear war as a metaphor for his recent emotional traumas. There were also some passing references to actress Diana Dors, whose death coincided with the writing of the composition. Other reference points included the reintroduction of harmonica, the old Caribbean inflexions and some closing bells recalling 'Big Black Smoke'. "There's some smart key changes in it," Ray noted. "There's four separate sections that work well, there's an apocalyptic moment. It was written and recorded very quickly, but it didn't come out until too late. As usual, if it had come out when I'd wanted it to it would have been a wonderful record for April or May."

LIVING ON A THIN LINE

The surprise return of Dave Davies as a singer-songwriter with the Kinks emphasized his growing need to find expression within the group. Those expecting some hard rock offering were pleasantly taken aback by this composition, which proved one of the best tracks on the album. An atmospheric opening

with acoustic and electric guitar was followed by a lyric alluding to the death of England's glories. It was a theme that most listeners would normally associate with the elder brother and proof positive that Dave could incorporate his work in the group without any sense of incongruity.

SOLD ME OUT

This was one of three songs on the album taken from Ray's extra-curricular project *Return To Waterloo*, a work which featured the current Kinks, minus Dave Davies. This was a simple but effective rock 'n' roll tune with Ray on harmonica and vocal.

MASSIVE REDUCTIONS

The deceptively jazzy opening suggested that this keyboards-dominated track might emerge as something special. Alas, it was average stuff with a lyric reiterating the old Davies theme of money worries in the wake of inflation.

GUILTY

Dave's second solo outing on the album sounded not unlike Roger Daltrey performing an early Seventies Who song. Although no match for 'Living On A Thin Line' it was an adequate filler for the album.

TOO HOT

With Gibbons' keyboard work evoking memories of 'Come Dancing', this should have been better, but ended up sounding half-baked. Ray was by now an avid exercise man and here used his workouts at the gym as an unlikely metaphor for the state of the nation. This track appeared as the flip side to the album's pilot single, 'Good Day'.

MISSING PERSONS

This was the second track borrowed from the film *Return To Waterloo*. Sensitively handled by Ray, it dealt with the anguish of parenthood and the difficulty of coming to terms with a missing girl. Although no 'She's Leaving Home', it was still one of the better tracks herein.

SUMMER'S GONE

This rather nondescript song was a surprise choice as a single. The theme recalled 'End Of The Season', albeit without the catchy melody. Ray at least provided an expressive vocal, but this wasn't his best material.

GOING SOLO

The album's concluding track was the third borrowing from *Return To Waterloo*. Like 'Missing Persons', the song deals with the loss of children and the resentment of parents when their young ones leave the nest. The song's title was an eyebrow-raising reminder of Ray's involvement in outside projects and a veiled hint that the history of the Kinks might be reaching its final chapter.

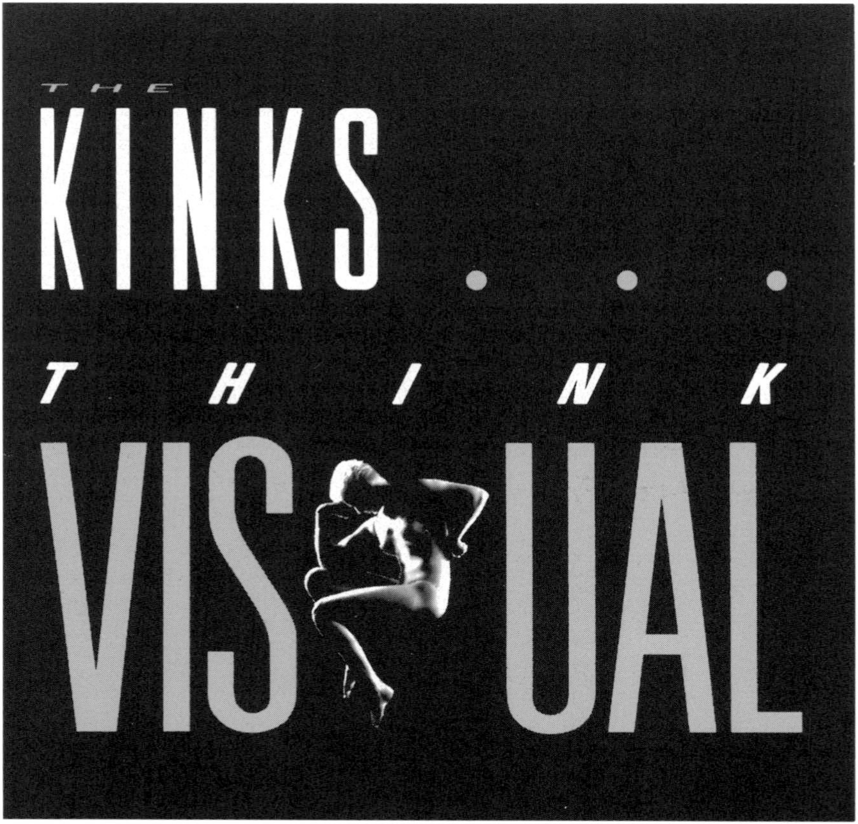
THE
KINKS . . .
THINK
VISUAL

THINK VISUAL

RELEASED: NOVEMBER 1986

ORIGINAL UK ISSUE: LONDON LONLP 27

This album was made under some duress and revealed Ray Davies at a new low of disillusionment. "My philosophy for this record was 'Nothing is as bad as I think it is'," he admitted. Given that viewpoint, it was not surprising to discover another frustratingly uneven record. On the plus side, the production was noticeably crisp and the songs well-executed. Unfortunately, the lyrical landscape offered a bleak and depressing view of the record industry and on several occasions Ray's songs laboured under the weight of a pre-ordained concept. Timing is crucial in pop and at this stage of their career, with their following in decline, the Kinks needed a very strong record to re-establish themselves commercially. This album had its moments and in some ways was a more interesting record than generally assumed, but it shared the flaws of so many of its predecessors: inconsistency. It was now clear that the Kinks needed something spectacular to forestall their decline into an unreconstituted oldies act and this was not that record. Predictably ignored in Britain, it peaked at number 81 in *Billboard*.

WORKING AT THE FACTORY

With a strong lead vocal from Ray and aggressive lead guitar work from Dave, this was one of the Kinks' most bitter indictments of the music business. Not since the scabrous *Lola Versus Powerman And The Moneygoround Part One* had they presented such a damning comment on the process of stardom. Davies documents the way in which pop offered him hope back in 1963, but goes on to present a sad account of disillusionment as big companies reduce artistes to the level of artisans. "Music should be art," he protested, in defence of the song.

LOST AND FOUND

With a strong dose of synthesizer creating the sound of steel drums and brass, Davies offers another strained metaphor – this time envisaging a hurricane as a symbol for his latest emotional upheaval. Not a particularly memorable song, but adequate in its context.

REPETITION

This was yet another reiteration of 'Predictable', with Ray portraying a personality reduced to the level of a product. The song included standard Kinks' riffs, sounding like a weak-kneed 'All Day And All Of The Night'.

WELCOME TO SLEAZY TOWN

This blues-based number, complete with harmonica, was another tirade against city developers, sung in an American accent. Although the much-maligned city was unnamed in the song, Davies later identified the concrete monstrosity as Cleveland. "You can't walk down Cleveland's main

street any more," he complained. "It used to be full of good shapes, but now there's only the occasional porn cinema. I wanted the song to about the American midwest, so that's why I adopted the accent."

THE VIDEO SHOP

Arguably the highlight of the album with a clever arrangement and catchy melody, this was a cut above virtually everything else on offer here. Davies imagines opening a video shop and feeding the masses with cheap counterfeit movies and porn. The fascination with the video format clearly captured Davies's imagination and he even suggested basing an entire musical on this one song. Needless to say, that idea was never developed.

ROCK & ROLL CITIES

In America, this was the first Kinks' A-side to emerge from the pen of Dave Davies. It was also the last song recorded for the album, having been completed at Konk back in London. Despite a promotional video and a radio-friendly feel, it failed to make any commercial impact. A rather clichéd and riff-heavy road song, it met an ambivalent response from the elder brother. "When I first heard that song, it made me sick," he confessed. "But then the next day I saw the humour in it."

HOW ARE YOU

This song of troubled communications between people was one of the better moments on the album. The conversational vocal was taken directly from Ray's original demo and the lead guitar sounded especially striking.

THINK VISUAL

The pop process is again investigated here, with Davies bemoaning marketing mania and the industry's tendency to place image before artistry. Unfortunately, this was not a notable song but rather a salutary comment on Davies's current predilection for sacrificing expression at the altar of didacticism.

NATURAL GIFT

This song was akin to a manual of self-improvement for an under-achiever, with

Ray singing in a voice disconcertingly similar to that of Lou Reed.

KILLING TIME

The evils of the leisure industry are again addressed here as Ray catalogues the time-wasting hours devoted to watching television. Interestingly, the couch potato couple described in the song were based on real acquaintances. "It's about a couple who haven't worked since they left school," he revealed. "They got up in the morning, turned on the television and just kept watching. That's something that fascinated me because it must affect the way you look at the world... 'Killing Time' is about the acceptance of the condition we're in."

WHEN YOU WERE A CHILD

Dave Davies's second offering on the album was tagged on at the end. In marked contrast to 'Rock & Roll Cities', this was a reflective melodic piece about uncorrupted childhood innocence. It neatly complemented Ray's more scathing, cynical observations about the state of modern life.

THE ROAD
(THE KINKS LIVE)

RELEASED: MAY 1988

ORIGINAL UK ISSUE: LONDON LONLP 49

It said much about the Kinks' current standing that this live album was initially issued in Germany, a full five months before its UK release. This was not a particularly welcome addition to the group's catalogue but served its purpose as a concert souvenir. The album actually began with a studio track, 'The Road', which was essentially a mini-history of the group. All the live tracks were previously released songs with the exception of 'It (I Want It)', a theatrical piece no doubt inspired by Ray's new wife Pat Crosbie, a ballet dancer whose choreographic skills were incorporated into the group's concert performances.

Full track listing: The Road; Destroyer; Apeman; Come Dancing; Art Lover; Cliches Of The World; Think Visual; Living On A Thin Line; Lost And Found; It (I Want It); Around The Dial; Give The People What They Want.

THE KINKS UK JIVE

UK JIVE

RELEASED: OCTOBER 1988

ORIGINAL UK ISSUE: LONDON 828. 165-2

By the time they released this album, the Kinks were in commercial freefall and could not even broach the US Top 100. Ray Davies was involved in a variety of outside projects and also at odds with his record company. The timing of the album's release turned out to be a disaster as the Kinks were unable or unwilling to schedule a tour to promote the record. It came and went amid further dissension within the group. By the end of the sessions, the affable keyboardist Ian Gibbons announced that he was leaving. "The atmosphere in the studio drove me away," he told me. "When they finally put the album out they didn't credit me, but I couldn't give a toss at the time." Given the continuing cold war between the brothers and all the problems surrounding the recording of the work, it would have been understandable if the results were disappointing. Ironically, what emerged from the chaos was probably the finest Kinks' album in nearly 20 years and undoubtedly one of their most severely underrated. Not since *Muswell Hillbillies* had they completed a work with such a strong selection of top tunes. Davies's songwriting was particularly impressive and there were many moments of melodic excellence scattered throughout the disc, reinforced by strong vocal work and impressive arrangements. As ever, a hit single and exceptionally good promotion were required to focus attention on the work, but neither was forthcoming. As the Eighties closed, the Kinks were at their lowest ebb commercially and, not surprisingly, left their latest record company amid considerable disillusionment.

AGGRAVATION

Like 'Pressure' and 'Repetition', this was another of Ray's one-word titled diatribes on the frustrations of modern-day life. Dave adds some dramatic lead-guitar fills while his brother's vocal performance becomes increasingly histrionic. Getting into character was uppermost in Ray's mind during the recording of the song. As he explained: "On 'Aggravation' the first thing that happens is the guy gets stuck in a traffic jam. Things just seem to go downhill from there. I delved into his personality and in the song I became him." The CD version of this track was an extended edit lasting over six minutes during which Dave was allowed some over-indulgence on his guitar solo.

HOW DO I GET CLOSE

One of the more poignant songs on the record, this spoke of designer feelings and emotional barrenness. Dave's playing was more melodic than usual, a far cry from the riff-dominated tracks heard earlier in the decade.

UK JIVE

An obvious single, this was probably the catchiest song on the album with its amusing doo-wop harmonies and irre-sistible chorus. Ray turns on his cockney accent to fine effect and it is gratifying to hear him using such archaic English phrases as "tallyman" and "never never" without worrying about translating the terms for a world audience. Amusingly, the song closes with a snatch of the Who's 'My Generation', neatly conjuring

up a golden era for both groups.

NOW AND THEN

The lyrics of this moving song are concerned with nothing less than the history of creation. In common with 'God's Children', it reflects on lost innocence and harks back to a time before the world was corrupted by big business. Essentially, this was a solo recording with Ray using a drum machine and overdubbing acoustic guitar.

WHAT ARE WE DOING

With its series of rhetorical questions and reflections on conformity, ecology and politics, this proved a zestful excur-sion made more urgent by a striking brass-based accompaniment. Ray's vocal is particularly expressive adding a much-needed drama to the proceedings.

ENTERTAINMENT

A late entry for the album, this track was originally recorded for *Give The People What They Want* at the beginning of the Eighties, but was replaced on that album by 'Better Things'. Unfortunately, it sounds terribly out of place here – a lumpy, leaden production, recalling the Kinks' more formulaic attempts to mould their sound for American AOR radio consumption.

WAR IS OVER

This pretty Beatlesque melody was the closest Ray had reached in re-creating the period feel of the Kinks' late Sixties work. Its pacifist theme and use of a military style brass band worked well and provided an impetus for the recording of the entire album. "I wrote the first line in desperation to get the guys something to rehearse," Ray explained. "The chords were tricky. It starts in A, which is not a very good key for me. We did a tricky thing in the mix. I sing the first verse melody on the harmony, then I bring in the octave singing the lead, building like a triad. We go to the chorus, which is fine, then we do a key change into my register, and from there I go for the melody. I told the band to think Merseybeat."

DOWN ALL THE DAYS (TILL 1992)

Although the title was borrowed from Christy Brown's brilliant autobiographical novel, this song had nothing to do with Ireland, but was intended to celebrate impending European unity. A superb single, which should have been a major hit, this was probably Davies's most exuberant and positive statement of the decade. "I'm losing all my bitterness," he exclaims at one point – and it shows. His anthem for the future featured an exultant lead vocal, reinforced by the sound of peeling bells and cheering crowds. This was the song that should have re-established the Kinks in the public imagination, but it was cruelly ignored. Keyboardist Mark Haley made his sole studio contribution on this track and would be long gone by the time they recorded their next album.

LOONY BALLOON

Another great melody from Davies, this was obviously inspired by Jules Vernes' *Around The World In 80 Days*. Ray had recently completed a musical *80 Days*, which he hoped might reach Broadway. Although this song was not featured in that project, its theme was clearly related. The rousing chorus contrasted brilliantly with the more downbeat social observations during the verses. A complex and engaging work, it underlined the quality still present in Davies's songwriting. An extended version appeared on the CD release.

DEAR MARGARET

One year after Morrissey had called for the death of the Prime Minister with the agit-prop 'Margaret On A Guillotine', Dave Davies released his own bile-ridden diatribe, marked by a vicious hard rock backing and a vocal laden with echo. At least Dave showed a peculiar sense of humour by recognizing the premier's sexuality with the cheeky line, "I like your wiggle when you walk".

BRIGHT LIGHTS

The vinyl version of *UK Jive* closed with 'Dear Margaret' but the CD release allowed Dave Davies a couple of extra tracks. This composition was a terribly clichéd hard rock number which sounded completely out of place on the record and merely demonstrated that the brothers were on different musical roads which were becoming increasingly irreconcilable.

PERFECT STRANGERS

According to Dave, he had to have a fist-fight with Ray before the elder brother agreed to allow this song to be included. It's actually better than either 'Dear Margaret' or 'Bright Lights' and some passion and intelligence is discernible beneath the bombastic approach. Clearly the CD age was working in Dave Davies's favour, although it was difficult to avoid the conclusion that he was being offered his own mini-album tucked safely away at the close of the work for fear of interfering with Ray's own statements.

PHOBIA

RELEASED: MARCH 1993

ORIGINAL UK ISSUE: COLUMBIA 4872489 2

After signing to a new record label, Columbia, the Kinks took an age to complete their next album. In October 1991, the company decided to release an interim 5 track CD, headed by 'Did Ya' and also including a live version of 'I Gotta Move', a remake of 'Days' and two otherwise unavailable tracks, 'New World' and Dave's 'Look Through Any Doorway'. Seventeen months later, *Phobia* was launched with a full publicity campaign in which Ray and Dave actively participated. Some good reviews were forthcoming and fans could not argue that the group weren't offering value for money on the CD, with 16 songs spread over 76 minutes. Unfortunately, quantity was rarely matched by quality. Although the Kinks were more focused on this project than on anything they had done in years, most of the songs were disappointingly average. Despite all the hype and hard work, it seemed that the Davies brothers were unable to save the work commercially. It reputedly sold a mere 5,000 copies in the UK, probably their worst-selling album of all time. In America, it graced the charts for just one week at number 166, their lowest chart-placing since *Preservation Act 1*, which had sold much more steadily over a longer period. There was no escaping the fact that the Kinks had hit an all-time low even while their profile was improving thanks to the Britpop explosion. At this point in their career, a more lyrical album featuring strong songs from Ray Davies might have kick-started a resurgence of interest in the Nineties, but the moment passed. The brothers drifted apart, the record company lost interest and as far as new studio work was concerned, the immediate future offered only silence.

OPENING

Dave Davies sets the scene with this 37-second instrumental, with shades of Jimi Hendrix.

WALL OF FIRE

The opening segues into this gruff-voiced hard rocker which sounds earnest enough thanks to a strong production, but offers little in the way of a decent melody and hardly ranks with Ray's better work.

DRIFT AWAY

The refrain of 'Loony Balloon' provides a promising introduction to this track, but it soon degenerates into another dull hard rock item. Thematically, it's another tired re-run of familiar Davies bugbears – the horrors of the world and the desire to escape into fantasy. The song was written back in 1990 during Britain's poll tax riots and Gulf War exploits. "I just felt all around me there was confusion in society," Davies reflected.

STILL SEARCHING

Changing the mood, Ray resurrects the tramp persona used extensively during the *Preservation* years for this escapist ballad. Although pleasant, this was less than riveting.

PHOBIA

The one-word title again indicates that this is another of those formulaic neurotic rants in the manner of 'Pressure' and 'Aggravation', only this time even more bombastic and minus any humorous observations.

ONLY A DREAM

This was a more original song of romantic wish-fulfilment in which a fantasy woman ("an executive goddess") is won and lost within the space of a couple of lift rides. It's hard to forgive the terrible concluding lines ("Life's just like that elevator/It takes you up and brings you down"), but at least the singing is impressive. As Ray pointed out: "I kind of found my voice on 'Only A Dream', which I wrote on a plane to England after I decided that the album needed to have a little more humanity."

DON'T

A keener grasp of melody was discernible on this intriguing tale of a man on a window ledge and his interaction with a voyeuristic audience below. Dave's guitar playing was also impressive in its subtlety. 'Don't' was the original title for the album and originally lasted almost nine minutes.

BABIES

Ray Davies's search for new neurotic themes reaches a comic peak here as he imagines the fears of a baby about to emerge from the womb. The group's performance recalled the Sixties' Kinks sound, with slight echoes of 'Till The End Of The Day'.

OVER THE EDGE

After quoting Shakespeare's "The world's a stage", Davies inevitably reflects on role-playing before offering some further social observations, culminating in an amusing tale about a deranged next-door neighbour. The melody was strikingly reminiscent of the Beatles' 'Dear Prudence'.

SURVIVING

This rampaging tribute to the art of survival was another nondescript rock workout, topped off by an atmospheric coda which ultimately threatened more than it provided.

IT'S ALRIGHT (DON'T THINK ABOUT IT)

Here was Dave Davies let loose to play some stereotypical heavy AOR material, complete with sub-Zeppelin riffs and an over the top apocalyptic theme. Almost a parody of the heavy metal genre, it evidently met with Ray's approval. "I really like 'It's Alright'," the elder brother admitted. "He's got the right to express himself; part of being in a band is to actually let the soloist solo."

THE INFORMER

Written during Ray's sojourn in Cork, this was one of the better tracks on the album, with a theme that echoed a musical he was working on during the same period. The cinematic feel was evident in the tale of an informer, on the run after betraying his comrades. "If you listen to the song, it has IRA connotations," Ray noted, "although I'm never that obvious as a writer. It doesn't mention the word assassination, but there's a subtext to the song."

HATRED (A DUET)

A welcome highlight came late in the album with this extraordinary duet in which the brothers attempt a psychodrama, verbally unleashing the intense mutual antipathy that has characterized their personal and professional relationship since the early days of the Kinks. "I wrote it for a two-headed transplant to sing as a split personality and then cast it as a duet as an afterthought," Ray noted. The power of song stems from its authenticity and the comic absurdity surrounding the Davies's seemingly perpetual love/hate saga.

SOMEBODY STOLE MY CAR

This derivative car song was a touch anticlimactic after 'Hatred' and another questionable inclusion. Like 'Over The Edge', it included a Beatles' musical reference, reprising the conclusion to 'Drive My Car'.

CLOSE TO THE WIRE

The spiritual side of Dave Davies's personality was in evidence here and it admittedly sounded much better than his hard rock efforts with some promising harmonies from Ray.

SCATTERED

An excellent single, perversely placed at the end of the album, this offered a strong melody and some moving lyrics, obviously inspired by the death of Ray and Dave's mother Annie Davies. Catchy and philosophical in tone, it demonstrated how good this album could have been under different circumstances.

DID YA

This bonus CD track had originally been issued as the lead track on the Kinks' 1991 5-track sampler. A wonderful pastiche of the mid-Sixties' Kinks, it included fond echoes of 'Sunny Afternoon' and some of Davies's more piercing, satirical lyrics. At a time when nostalgia for the Swinging Sixties was back in vogue, Ray took a scalpel to the era and tore into the utopian nostalgia with an insouciant, sardonic glee. 'Where Have All The Good Times Gone?' had offered a similar message, but this is far more caustic and sarcastic and all the better for it. Relegated to a tag-on track here, it easily eclipsed the majority of the preceding songs.

TO THE BONE

RELEASED: OCTOBER 1994

ORIGINAL UK ISSUE: KONK/GRAPEVINE KNKLP 1

This live album was a part electric/part acoustic set borrowed from various sources. 'Apeman', 'Tired Of Waiting', 'See My Friend' and 'Death Of A Clown' were recorded live before a specially invited audience of Kinks' fans at London's Konk Studios on 11 April 1994. There were also Ray Davies's solo live versions of 'Autumn Almanac', 'Sunny Afternoon' and 'Dedicated Follower Of Fashion', a group version of 'All Day All Of The Night', reputedly recorded at the Guildhall, Portsmouth on 25 March 1994, and a finale of 'You Really Got Me' taken from a show at the Mann Music Center, Philadelphia, PA on 12 August 1993. Overall, these selections served to create a reminder of the impressive pedigree of the Kinks as a recording and performing unit. Unfortunately, there would be no immediate follow-up studio album to take advantage of the renewed interest in the group following the Britpop explosion.

Full track listing: All Day And All Of The Night; Apeman; Tired Of Waiting; See My Friend; Death Of A Clown; Waterloo Sunset; Muswell Hillbillies; Better Things; Don't Forget To Dance; Autumn Almanac; Sunny Afternoon; Dedicated Follower Of Fashion; You Really Got Me.

TO THE BONE

RELEASED: MARCH 1997 (US RELEASE OCTOBER 1996)

ORIGINAL UK ISSUE: GUARDIAN 7243 837303 21

This much superior update of *To The Bone* was a radically reworked version of the 1994 version. Most of the original set was retained with the exception of 'Waterloo Sunset' and 'Autumn Almanac', replaced by two versions of 'Do It Again'. A second disc featured some startling new live material, highlighted by several surprise selections from *The Kinks Are The Village Green Preservation Society*, including an amusing "Bavarian version" of 'Do You Remember Walter' slowed down with an accordion backing. A bluesy 'Set Me Free', sprightly 'Come Dancing' and downbeat 'I'm Not Like Everybody Else' were also featured. The work concluded with two previously unreleased songs: 'Animal', the story of an often abusive relationship ending in divorce and 'To The Bone', an Eastern-flavoured acoustic number whose underlying theme reflected on the potency of old records in evoking past memories.

Full track listing: All Day And All Of The Night; Apeman; Tired Of Waiting; See My Friend; Death Of A Clown; Muswell Hillbillies; Better Things; Don't Forget To Dance; Sunny Afternoon; Dedicated Follower Of Fashion; Do It Again (acoustic); Do It Again; Celluloid Heroes; Picture Book; Village Green Preservation Society; Do You Remember Walter; Set Me Free; Lola; Come Dancing; I'm Not Like Everybody Else; Till The End Of The Day; Give The People What They Want; State Of Confusion; Dead End Street; A Gallon Of Gas; Days; You Really Got Me; Animal; To The Bone.

COMPILATIONS

As I emphasized in the introduction to the Singles section, the number of hits and general compilation albums issued by the Kinks is vast. During the Sixties, Pye recycled the group's recordings on their budget Golden Guinea and Marble Arch labels and in the Seventies issued several on the *Golden Hour* series. When Pye was sold off, PRT and subsequently Castle Communications continued to churn out more product, even leasing the stuff to other labels. The result has been a saturation of Kinks' material in the marketplace, a trend that has continued even during the CD age. Although the reissues have covered every conceivable aspect of the Kinks' recording career, precious little new material has emerged in the UK. The 1993 album, *The Kinks Greatest/Dead End Street* (PRT Kinks 1) did feature a bonus 10-inch LP containing some oddities, including 'Misty Water', 'Pictures In The Sand' and 'Groovy Movies' (see *The Great Lost Kinks Album* in the next section for full details of these tracks), plus the unissued and incomplete 'Time Will Tell' and a warm-up number, 'Spotty Grotty Anna'. Remaining compilations have merely repeated old and familiar tracks *ad infinitum*. Space precludes titles and track listing details for these endless compilations, but those seeking a definitive listing (including all variants throughout the world!) are strongly advised to invest in Doug Hinman's *You Really Got Me: An Illustrated World Discography Of The Kinks, 1964-1993*, available from PO Box 4759, Rumford, Rhode Island 02916-0759, USA.

ANOMALOUS AMERICAN ARCHIVAL ALBUMS

Although this discography specializes in UK releases, mention must be made of two US releases that feature otherwise rare or unavailable material. Reprise Records generally took their lead from the UK Pye releases but, following the Kinks' defection to RCA, they elected to clear their tape shelves and issue a couple of archival albums.

THE KINKS KRONIKLES

RELEASED: MARCH 1972
ORIGINAL ISSUE: REPRISE 2XS 6454 (US ONLY)

This exciting compilation featured many recordings previously available on B-side only and completely new to American listeners. There were also exclusive stereo mixes of several crucial songs, most notably 'Autumn Almanac' and 'Susannah's Still Alive'. One previously unissued track was also made available: 'Did You See His Name?'

Full track listing: Victoria; The Village Green Preservation Society; Berkeley Mews; Holiday In Waikiki; Willesden Green; This Is Where I Belong; Waterloo Sunset; David Watts; Dead End Street; Shangri-la; Autumn Almanac; Sunny Afternoon; Get Back In Line; Did You See His Name?; Fancy; Wonderboy; Apeman; King Kong; Mister Pleasant; God's Children; Death Of A Clown; Lola; Mindless Child Of Motherhood; Polly; Big Black Smoke; Susannah's Still Alive; She's Got Everything; Days.

THE GREAT LOST KINKS ALBUM

RELEASED: JANUARY 1973
ORIGINAL ISSUE: REPRISE MS 2127 (US ONLY)

Reprise's decision to reject the *Percy* soundtrack as a legitimate release meant that they were still due one more album from the Kinks. In the absence of new product, they made the controversial decision to release this item, which featured various rarities, including a number of unreleased tracks, mostly in demo form. The record was deleted within two years of release following objections from Ray Davies and has never appeared on CD. Among the key rarities were the following:

TILL DEATH US DO PART

Ray Davies was commissioned to write a song for the movie *Till Death Us Do Part*, based on the popular BBC comedy series of the mid-Sixties. The film version featured an uncredited Kinks backing track, with Chas Mills on lead vocal. This original demo version was an attractive piece with trombone backing and thoughtful lyrics from Davies.

LAVENDER HILL

Despite the primitive recording quality, this was an attractive piece immortalizing another London place name, previously made famous via the film, *The Lavender Hill Mob*. The tone of the piece has strong stylistic echoes of 'Dead End Street'.

GROOVY MOVIES

This was one of the songs intended for Dave Davies's 1969 solo album. It's a catchy number with Dave imagining himself as a film-maker. An alternate version was included on the 1983 UK compilation, *The Kinks' Greatest Hits/Dead End Street*.

ROSEMARY ROSE

The title suggests that this may have been another of Ray's passing tributes to his sister Rose. A harpsichord backing was to be added to the track and it would have made a reasonable addition to *The Kinks Are The Village Green Preservation Society* or *Arthur*. It later appeared on the UK issue: *The Kinks' Greatest Hits/Dead End Street*.

MISTY WATER

This slight track probably required considerably more work, but it was a pretty melody, with Davies acknowledging his love of fog and haze. Again, UK listeners could sample the track on *The Kinks' Greatest Hits/Dead End Street*.

MR SONGBIRD

Technically, this was not a rarity as it had already featured on Continental editions of *The Kinks Are The Village Green Preservation Society*. However, it remained unreleased in Britain, not even appearing on a B-side. A charming lilt, with a flute accompaniment, it was a light and delicate piece, hardly crucial but most attractive.

WHEN I TURN OUT THE LIVING ROOM LIGHT

An example of Ray's dark humour, this anti-romantic song was a lyrical equivalent of the proverb, "All cats are grey in the dark". Davies takes delight in cataloguing a lover's physical shortcomings – bulbous nose, wrinkled skin – before adding that ugliness disappears once the lights are turned off. The song briefly appeared on the 1970 American Various Artistes' collection *The Big Ball,* but was otherwise unavailable. Its limited release and general obscurity probably saved Ray from belatedly misguided accusations of anti-Semitism. Daringly, he opened the composition with the questionable line "Who cares if you're Jewish?", as if suggesting that the state of being a Jew was itself an unattractive trait.

PICTURES IN THE SAND

There was a touch of Noel Coward about this tribute to the seaside, which offered a distinctly 1920s musical feel. A non-vocal version of this track subsequently appeared on the UK compilation *The Kinks' Greatest Hits/Dead End Street*.

WHERE DID MY SPRING GO

During 1969, Ray Davies was commissioned to write a song a week for the six-part BBC satire programme *Where Was Spring?*, which featured Eleanor Bron. Among the songs reputedly included were 'Did You See His Name?', 'Darling I Respect You', 'Let's Take Off All Our Clothes' and the aforementioned 'When I Turn Out The Living Room Light'. The key song for the series was clearly 'Where Did My Spring Go?', a dark reflection on age, ill health and decay with Ray echoing Shakespeare's Jacques in his gloomy but philosophical vision of approaching death: sans hair, sans skin, sans bones, sans everything.

Full track listing: Till Death Us Do Part; There Is No Life Without Love; Lavender Hill; Groovy Movies; Rosemary Rose; Misty Water; Mr Songbird; When I Turn Out The Living Room Light; The Way Love Used To Be; I'm Not Like Everybody Else; Plastic Man; This Man He Weeps Tonight; Pictures In The Sand; Where Did My Spring Go.

DAVE DAVIES RECORDINGS
SINGLES - THE PYE YEARS

DEATH OF A CLOWN/ LOVE ME TILL THE SUN SHINES

RELEASED: AUGUST 1967

ORIGINAL UK ISSUE: PYE 7N 17356

Dave Davies began his solo career in spectacular fashion with this massive summer hit, which threatened to establish him as a singer in his own right. Despite a memorable appearance on *Top Of The Pops*, he seemed reluctant to allow his extra-curricular work to interfere with Kinks' commitments. There was also confusion as to what differentiated a Dave Davies recording from a Kinks recording. Both sides of this disc were also included on *Something Else By The Kinks*, confirming the younger brother's rather contradictory role as both a soloist and group member.

SUSANNAH'S STILL ALIVE/FUNNY FACE

RELEASED: NOVEMBER 1967

ORIGINAL UK ISSUE: PYE 7N 17429

Proving that he was no one hit wonder, Dave wrote another strong single, this time about a frustrated girl "who has no luck with the blokes". This rivalled some of the Kinks' best work of the period with a great bass line, pumping piano, intriguing lyrics and a suitably dramatic vocal. It reached the Top 20, but deserved to fare much better. The B-side was another Dave composition, again borrowed from *Something Else By The Kinks*.

DAVE DAVIES HITS (EP)
RELEASED: APRIL 1968
ORIGINAL UK ISSUE: PYE NEP 24289

Pye wasted no time in collating the first four sides of Dave's solo career for a premature, but nevertheless rewarding EP, with a running order: 'Love Me Till The Sun Shines'; 'Death Of A Clown'; 'Susannah's Still Alive'; 'Funny Face'.

LINCOLN COUNTY/THERE IS NO LIFE WITHOUT LOVE
RELEASED: AUGUST 1968
ORIGINAL PYE ISSUE: 7N 17514

Released two months earlier in Holland, the third Dave Davies single was his first commercial failure. Backed by an array of instrumentation, including strings, this celebration of freedom from a jail sentence was every bit as ambitious as Dave's first two singles, but a lack of radio airplay sealed its doom. The flip side, a slight but quaint ballad sung like a mantra, provided a suitable accompaniment.

HOLD MY HAND/ CREEPING JEAN
RELEASED: JANUARY 1969
ORIGINAL UK ISSUE: PYE 7N 17678

Dave Davies's promising solo career was blighted by the unheralded release of his final single of the era – the mournful 'Hold My Hand'. Musically and vocally, the work betrayed the influence of Dylan and the Band, but Dave's strained singing was off-putting. This was eminently uncommercial and, not surprisingly, failed to chart. The B-side was much better with its jingle-jangle guitar, gulping bass line and odd, almost indecipherable lyrics.

So ended the Sixties' singles career of Dave Davies. It would be another 11 years before he returned, but by that time the era of the exclusive singles release would be largely over. Later releases with RCA and Warner Brothers were all included on albums of the period.

ALBUMS

The prospect of a Dave Davies solo album was a much-anticipated event during the late Sixties. It was announced that he intended to tour and was in the process of completing a work for release in 1969, but after the failure of 'Hold My Hand', Pye Records appeared to lose interest in the project. Unlike many unrealized ventures, the Dave Davies album was always tantalizingly close to fruition. An acetate from the period reveals a seemingly completed track listing, comprising 'Susannah's Still Alive', 'There Is No Life Without Love', 'This Man He Weeps Tonight', 'Mindless Child Of Motherhood', 'Hold My Hand', 'Do You Wish To Be A Man', 'Are You Ready', 'Creeping Jean', 'Crying', 'Lincoln County', 'Mr Shoemaker's Daughter', 'Mr Reporter' and 'Groovy Movies'. The record looked extremely promising on paper and might have helped Dave establish an artistic outlet away from the overbearing artistic presence of his brother. Instead, the work was postponed, then abandoned. For most of the Seventies, Dave's creativity was stifled by Ray's determination to pursue theatrical works under the banner of the Kinks. Amazingly, it would not be until 1980 that the younger brother finally released the album that had been promised 13 years before.

PL 13603 (Dave Davies)

RELEASED: SEPTEMBER 1980
ORIGINAL UK ISSUE: RCA PL 13603

Probably the most original aspect of this album was the decision to title the work after its serial number, although UK copies are usually referred to under the artiste title *Dave Davies*. The US version, released two months before, was unambiguously called *AFLI-3603*. For those of us patiently awaiting something to match the legendary unreleased album from the Sixties, this was a bitter disappointment. The work of baroque ballads, strong melodies and impressive arrangements that might have been forthcoming a decade before was instead replaced by a predictably banal heavy metal album. In many ways, this new work resembled an exercise in retaliatory frustration after years of having to play alongside brass bands and chorus lines in brother Ray's increasingly cyclical theatrical musicals.

Full track listing: Where Do You Come From; Doing The Best For You; Visionary Dreamer; Nothing More To Lose; The World Is Changing Hands; Move Over; See The Beast; Imagination's Real; In You I Believe; Run.

arrangements and musical bombast. Not surprisingly, this work ended Dave's short-lived career as a solo artiste on RCA.

Full track listing: Is This The Only Way; Glamour; Reveal Yourself; World Of Our Own; Body; Too Serious; Telepathy; 7th Channel; Eastern Eyes.

GLAMOUR
RELEASED: OCTOBER 1981
ORIGINAL UK ISSUE: RCA LP 6005

If anything, this was even more cacophonous than its predecessor, with Dave seemingly determined to match the loudness of a Led Zeppelin record, albeit without their melodic ingenuity or decent song structures. Even Dave later conceded that it was "too raw" but seemed convinced that it was the record's supposedly aggressive political stance as much as its sound that caused offence. It's doubtful whether too many listeners gleaned the lyrics beneath the leaden

CHOSEN PEOPLE
RELEASED: OCTOBER 1983
ORIGINAL UK ISSUE:
WARNER BROTHERS 92-3917-1

Dave's final newly-recorded solo album to date was thankfully a considerable improvement upon the two RCA LPs. This time, he mixed the hard rock numbers with some more reflective ballads and fashioned a more rounded work. It was an age away from 'Death Of A Clown', but most Kinks followers would probably maintain that his best work as a solo artiste was lost on that abandoned album at the close of the Sixties.

Full track listing: Tapas; Charity; Mean

Disposition; Love Gets You; Danger Zone; True Story; Take One More Chance; Freedom Lies; Matter Of Decision; Is It Any Wonder; Fire Burning; Chosen People; Cold Winter.

THE ALBUM THAT NEVER WAS
RELEASED: OCTOBER 1987
ORIGINAL UK ISSUE: PRT PYL 6012

Despite the tantalizing title, this was not a belated release of Dave's mythic Sixties solo album, but a clever rounding up of his first four solo singles in one package, neatly topped up with a couple of his B-side Kinks' compositions.

Full track listing: Death Of A Clown; Love Me Till The Sun Shines; Susannah's Still Alive; Funny Face; Lincoln County; There Is No Life Without Love; Hold My Hand; Creeping Jean; Mindless Child Of Motherhood; This Man He Weeps Tonight.

RAY DAVIES RECORDINGS

Rumours of a Ray Davies solo album began as early as 1967, but until relatively recently he seemed unwilling to step outside the secure aegis of the Kinks. The following documents the elder brother's extra-curricular recording activities to date registered under his own name.

RETURN TO WATERLOO
RELEASED: JULY 1985 (US ONLY)
ORIGINAL ISSUE: ARISTA AL6 8386

The soundtrack to Ray Davies's television film *Return To Waterloo* was unissued in the UK, but received a US release. Three of the songs from the film were also featured on the Kinks' *Word Of Mouth*, while two compositions remain unissued: 'Good Times Are Gone' and 'Ladder Of Success'.

Full track listing: Introduction; Return To Waterloo; Going Solo; Missing Persons; Sold Me Out; Dear Lonely Hearts; Not Far Away; Expectations; Voices In The Dark.

ABSOLUTE BEGINNERS
RELEASED: MARCH 1986
ORIGINAL UK ISSUE: VIRGIN V 2386

The soundtrack to this film included the Ray Davies cameo 'Quiet Life', one of the best musical moments in the film. This track was subsequently issued as a single in the UK backed with 'Voices In The Dark'.

THE SONGS OF RAY DAVIES WATERLOO SUNSET
RELEASED: SEPTEMBER 1997
ORIGINAL UK ISSUE: ESSENTIAL ESS CD 592

The publication of Ray Davies's short story collection *Waterloo Sunset* inspired this intriguing but motley compilation of demos and original tracks. The 15-track selection was included as a bonus disc

with *The Kinks: The Singles Collection*, complete with liner notes from Ray. As well as remixes of 'Voices In The Dark' and 'Art Lover', the album boasted three unreleased tracks: 'The Shirt', an outtake from the Kinks' first Arista album; the odd satire on real estate prices 'The-Million-Pound-Semi-Detached'; and the introspective 'My Diary'.

Full track listing: The Shirt: Rock And Roll Fantasy; Mr Pleasant; Celluloid Heroes; Voices In The Dark; Holiday Romance; Art Lover; Still Searching; Return To Waterloo; Afternoon Tea; The Million-Pound-Semi-Detached; My Diary; Drivin'; Waterloo Sunset; Scattered.

THE STORYTELLER
RELEASED: MARCH 1998
ORIGINAL UK ISSUE: EMI 494 1682

The Storyteller series of concerts began in March 1995, initially under the title *Ray Davies: 20th Century Man*. The idea was for Ray to promote his book *X-Ray* by reading extracts interspersed with a selection of his greatest songs, with backing from acoustic/electric guitarist Pete Mathison. The prospect of hearing some of the Kinks' best work in an acoustic format, complete with lengthy song introductions and amusing anecdotes, proved an unexpected treat. Among the highlights were moving readings of 'Set Me Free' and 'See My Friends', plus a Delta blues version of 'You Really Got Me', which boasted the presence of drummer Bobby Graham who played on the original Pye recording. Davies's stories of his home life and early days were often revealing and for those familiar with the Kinks' saga, the humorous reflections on Mick Avory, Larry Page, Grenville Collins and Robert Wace were hugely entertaining. Even the new songs did not disappoint, with 'The Ballad Of Julie Finkle' emerging as a high point. Although a project such as this could only be attempted once on record, the live record augured well for a future Ray Davies studio album.

Full track listing: Storyteller; Introduction; Victoria; My Name (Dialogue); 20th Century Man; London Song; My Big Sister (Dialogue); That Old Black Magic; Tired Of Waiting; Set Me Free (Instrumental); Dad And The Green Amp (Dialogue); Set Me Free; The Front Room (Dialogue); See My Friends; Autumn Almanac; Hunchback (Dialogue); X-Ray; Art School (Dialogue); Art School Babe; Back In The Front Room; Writing The Song (Dialogue); When Big Bill Speaks/The Man Who Knew A Man (Mick Avory's Audition – Dialogue); It's Alright (Managers – Dialogue); It's Alright (Havana Version, The Kinks Name – Dialogue); It's Alright (Uptempo, On The Road – Dialogue); Julie Finkle (Dialogue); The Ballad Of Julie Finkle; The Third Single (Dialogue); You Really Got Me; London Song (Studio Version).

REMASTERED REISSUES

Unlike their great contemporaries, the Kinks have yet to be afforded a box set release and, up until recently, their greatest work was still being recycled from later generation tapes. The need for a thorough reissue programme was paramount and once Ray Davies agreed to become involved in remastering their original Pye albums, some decent product was at last available to long-suffering aficionados. At the time of writing, the first five Kinks' studio albums have been reissued with a further batch due later in 1998. With an array of additional bonus tracks, the albums at last provide a more rounded picture of the Kinks as recording artistes, taking in classic singles and EP tracks to add glitter to the grist. In several cases, lesser albums have been transformed by the quality of the additional material, providing new listeners with a comprehensive view of the group in all their glory. With the Pye excavation completed, the next stage of remastering will feature the RCA years, with releases scheduled for the second half of 1998.

THE SINGLES COLLECTION
RELEASED: SEPTEMBER 1997
ORIGINAL UK ISSUE: ESSENTIAL ESS CD 592

The long-awaited remastering of the Kinks' Pye catalogue was premiered by the release of *The Singles Collection*. On the sleeve Ray Davies takes credit for "production", with Shel Talmy's name omitted entirely, even from the small print detailing publishing credits and dates.

Although this collection cannot extinguish the memory of countless other Kinks' hit compilations, it remains the one hits collection on which Davies appears to have been actively involved both in remastering the tapes and giving the project his blessing. Such approval was conditional upon the surprise inclusion of a second disc inspired by his book of short stories, Waterloo Sunset (see *The Songs Of Ray Davies Waterloo Sunset* in the Ray Davies Solo Recordings section).

Hearing the golden age of the Kinks across successive A-sides, including Dave Davies's first two solo singles, provides a pleasing reminder of their contribution towards Sixties' pop music.

Full track listing: Long Tall Sally; You Still Want Me; You Really Got Me; All Day And All Of The Night; Tired Of Waiting For You; Ev'rybody's Gonna Be Happy; Set Me Free; See My Friend; Till The End Of The Day; Where Have All The Good Times Gone; Dedicated Follower Of Fashion; A Well Respected Man; Sunny Afternoon; Dead End Street; Waterloo Sunset; Death Of A Clown; Autumn Almanac; David Watts; Susannah's Still Alive; Wonderboy; Days; Plastic Man; Victoria; Lola; Apeman. [For contents of Disc Two see The Songs Of Ray Davies Waterloo Sunset*).*

KINKS
RELEASED: APRIL 1998
ORIGINAL UK ISSUE: ESSENTIAL ESS CD 482

Like some of the other remastered albums in this first batch of Kinks' reissues, the original work was partly eclipsed by the generous selection of bonus tracks, which included the group's first three singles, the entire *Kinksize Sessions* EP, an unreleased take of 'Too Much Monkey Business' and the previously unissued beat pastiche 'I Don't Need You Anymore'. The presence of 'All Day And All Of The Night' in the revised listing adds depth to a memorable, if chaotic, debut album. With 12 extra tracks, taking the total up to 26 songs, this is an indispensable bargain.

Full track listing: Beautiful Delilah; So Mystifying; Just Can't Go To Sleep; Long Tall Shorty; I Took My Baby Home; I'm A Lover Not A Fighter; You Really Got Me; Cadillac; Bald Headed Woman; Revenge; Too Much Monkey Business; I've Been Driving On Bald Mountain; Stop Your Sobbin'; Got Love If You Want It; Long Tall Sally; You Still Want Me; You Do Something To Me; It's Alright; All Day And All Of The Night; I Gotta Move; Louie, Louie; I Gotta Go Now; Things Are

Getting Better; I've Got That Feeling; Too Much Monkey Business (Unreleased Alternate Take); I Don't Need You Anymore (Previously Unreleased).

KINDA KINKS
RELEASED: APRIL 1998
ORIGINAL UK ISSUE: ESSENTIAL ESS CD 483

A classic example of a cash-in album on its original release, the remastered reissue is literally transformed by the inclusion of the 11 bonus tracks, which serve as an additional album in itself and one that is superior to its parent release. Here, the Kinks make history by eclipsing their own original album with contemporaneous cuts that provide an embarrassment of riches. As well as several class singles, there's the highly-regarded *Kwyet Kinks* EP and one breathtakingly excellent unreleased gem – a Ray Davies publishing demo of 'I Go To Sleep'. Listening to the quality of this track, you immediately realize why Peggy Lee and others agreed to record this strong Davies composition. The fact that the Kinks themselves failed to include the

song on any album, while pursuing obviously inferior material is all part of the perverse story.

Full track listing: Look For Me Baby; Got My Feet On The Ground; Nothin' In The World Can Stop Me Worryin' About That Girl; Naggin' Woman; Wonder Where My Baby Is Tonight; Tired Of Waiting For You; Dancing In The Street; Don't Ever Change; Come On Now; So Long; You Shouldn't Be Sad; Something Better Beginning; Ev'rybody's Gonna Be Happy; Who'll Be The Next In Line; Set Me Free; I Need You; See My Friend; Never Met A Girl Like You Before; Wait Till The Summer Comes Along; Such A Shame; A Well Respected Man; Don't You Fret; I Go To Sleep (Unreleased Demo Recording).

THE KINK KONTROVERSY
RELEASED: APRIL 1998
ORIGINAL UK ISSUE: ESSENTIAL ESS CD 507

Bonus tracks were in short supply for this remastered reissue and as a result the original is boosted by only four additional items, including a rough unreleased publishing demo of 'When I See That Girl Of Mine' and an alternate take of 'Dedicated Follower Of Fashion', complete with tinkling piano. As a result, this album now replaces *Kinda Kinks* as the least attractive work in the group's Sixties canon.

Full track listing: Milk Cow Blues; Ring The Bells; Gotta Get The First Plane Home; When I See That Girl Of Mine; I Am Free; Till The End Of The Day; The World Keeps Going Round; I'm On An Island; Where Have All The Good Times Gone; It's Too Late; What's In Store For Me; You Can't Win; Dedicated Follower Of Fashion; Sittin' On My Sofa; When I See That Girl Of Mine (Unreleased Demo Recording); Dedicated Follower Of Fashion (Unreleased Alternate Stereo Take).

FACE TO FACE
RELEASED: APRIL 1998
ORIGINAL UK ISSUE: ESSENTIAL ESS CD 479

What was undoubtedly the first really strong album in the Kinks' canon and one of their most memorable of the Sixties is

here transformed into indisputable greatness by a towering selection of bonus tracks, including two of the finest B-sides of the era, 'I'm Not Like Everybody Else' and 'Big Black Smoke'. The startling 'Dead End Street' and export-only single 'Mister Pleasant' sound as biting as ever in their new context. 'This Is Where I Belong', originally the Continental B-side of 'Mister Pleasant' is an intriguing fusion of Sixties' psychedelic pop with Davies's reflections on home comforts. The legendary 'Mr Reporter' sounds like Dylan protest transmuted through English dated brass, with Dave Davies at his sneering best. Finally, there is a fascinating stereo backing track for the otherwise unissued 'Little Women', which sounds positively tantalizing.

Full track listing: Party Line; Rosie Won't You Please Come Home; Dandy; Too Much On My Mind; Session Man; Rainy Day In June; A House In The Country; Holiday In Waikiki; Most Exclusive Residence For Sale; Fancy; Little Miss Queen Of Darkness; You're Looking Fine; Sunny Afternoon; I'll Remember; I'm

Not Like Everybody Else; Dead End Street; Big Black Smoke; Mister Pleasant; This Is Where I Belong; Mr Reporter (Previously Unreleased); Little Women (Previously Unreleased Backing Track).

SOMETHING ELSE BY THE KINKS
RELEASED: APRIL 1998
ORIGINAL UK ISSUE: ESSENTIAL ESS CD 480

This classic album was already arguably the finest collection of individual Kinks songs placed on a single official LP. The bonus tracks serve to improve Dave Davies's standing from the period with reminders of his solo singles 'Susannah's Still Alive' and 'Lincoln County'. 'Days' was originally anticipated among the bonus tracks, but was removed from this selection without explanation. It would have been fascinating to have heard some unreleased songs or radically different takes from this precious period, but all we get is a remixed version of 'Lazy Old

Sun'. Perhaps the vaults were empty, but it seems more likely that Ray declined to sanction the inclusion of still unheard demos and songwriting experiments from this fertile period. A future box set might throw further light on this stage of the Kinks' career.

Full track listing: David Watts; Death Of A Clown; Two Sisters; No Return; Harry Rag; Tin Soldier Man; Situation Vacant; Love Me Till The Sun Shines; Lazy Old Sun; Afternoon Tea; Funny Face; End Of The Season; Waterloo Sunset; Act Nice And Gentle; Autumn Almanac; Susannah's Still Alive; Wonderboy; Polly; Lincoln County; There's No Life Without Love; Lazy Old Sun (Unreleased Alternate Stereo Take).

LIVE AT KELVIN HALL
RELEASED: MAY 1998
ORIGINAL UK ISSUE: ESSENTIAL ESM CD 508

The CD reissue features the original mono issue, plus a complete stereo version as a bonus. Alas, no new live tracks were forthcoming from any source.

Full track listing: [The mono album] 'Till The End Of The Day', 'A Well Respected Man', 'You're Looking Fine', 'Sunny Afternoon', 'Dandy', 'I'm On An Island', 'Come On Now', 'You Really Got Me', 'Medley: Milk Cow Blues, Batman Theme, Tired Of Waiting For You'. [The stereo album] 'Till The End Of The Day', 'A Well Respected Man', 'You're Looking Fine', 'Sunny Afternoon', 'Dandy', 'I'm On An Island', 'Come On Now', 'You Really Got Me', 'Medley: Milk Cow Blues, Batman Theme, Tired Of Waiting For You'.

THE KINKS ARE THE VILLAGE GREEN PRESERVATION SOCIETY
RELEASED: MAY 1998
ORIGINAL UK ISSUE: ESSENTIAL ESM CD 481

The remastered CD of this stupendous album initially disappoints as no new bonus songs are forthcoming. Instead we get the original mono album, plus the 12-track stereo Continental issue which featured the stereo 'Days'. Finally, there is the mono single version of 'Days' for completists.

Full track listing: [The Mono Album] The Village Green Preservation Society; Do You Remember Walter; Picture Book; Johnny Thunder; Last Of The Steam-Powered Trains; Big Sky; Sitting By The Riverside; Animal Farm; Village Green Starstruck; Phenomenal Cat; All Of My Friend Were There; Wicked Annabella; Monica; People Take Pictures Of Each Other. [The Stereo Album] The Village Green Preservation Society; Do You

Remember Walter; Picture Book; Johnny Thunder; Monica; Days; Village Green; Mr Songbird; Wicked Annabella; Starstruck; Phenomenal Cat; People Take Pictures Of Each Other. Days (mono single).

ARTHUR OR THE DECLINE AND FALL OF THE BRITISH EMPIRE

RELEASED: MAY 1998

ORIGINAL UK ISSUE: ESSENTIAL ESM CD 511

The 10 bonus tracks included at the end of this CD round up the Kinks' A&B-sides of the period in both their mono and stereo issues. As with its predecessor, new songs from this most fertile period are at a premium. Thankfully, Dave Davies's 'Mr Shoemaker's Daughter', a track scheduled from his doomed 1969 solo album has been unearthed. With its Byrds-like 'Feel A Whole Lot Better' opening and general folk-rock feel, the track was another reminder of a work sadly lost.

Full track listing: Victoria; Yes Sir, No Sir; Drivin'; Brainwashed; Australia; Shangri-la; Mr Churchill Says; She Bought A Hat Like Princess Marina; Young And Innocent Days; Nothing To Say; Arthur; Plastic Man (mono); King Kong (mono); Drivin' (mono); Mindless Child Of Motherhood (mono); This Man He Weeps Tonight (mono); Plastic Man (stereo); Mindless Child Of Motherhood (stereo); This Man He Weeps Tonight (stereo); She Bought A Hat Like Princess Marina (mono); Mr Shoemaker's Daughter (previously unreleased).

THE KINKS PART ONE – LOLA VERSUS POWERMAN AND THE MONEYGOROUND

RELEASED: MAY 1998

ORIGINAL UK ISSUE: ESSENTIAL ESM CD 509

As we reach the end of the Kinks' years with Pye, the bonus tracks become more scarce. All we get here is the single version of 'Lola', a demo of 'Apeman' with some Chuck Berry riffs in the mid-section and a demo of 'Powerman' offering little surprises.

Full track listing: The Contenders; Strangers; Denmark Street; Get Back In The Line; Lola; Top Of The Pops; The Moneygoround; This Time Tomorrow; A Long Way From Home; Rats; Apeman; Powerman; Got To Be Free; Lola (single version); Apeman (demo); Powerman (demo).

PERCY

RELEASED: MAY 1998

ORIGINAL UK ISSUE: ESSENTIAL ESM CD 510

Nobody was expecting anything special to be added to the *Percy* CD. The booklet does contain some colour stills from the film and there are five unreleased alternate mixes, comprising 'Dreams' (shorter version, minus the group's backing), 'Moments' (a 42-second instrumental fragment) and three versions of 'The Way Love Used To Be' (orchestral; vocal, and instrumental takes).

Full track listing: God's Children; Lola (Instrumental); The Way Love Used To Be; Completely; Running Round Town; Moments; Animals In The Zoo; Just Friends; Whip Lady; Dreams; Helga; Willesden Green; God's Children (End); Dreams; Moments; The Way Love Used To Be; The Way Love Used To Be; The Way Love Used To Be.

INDEX